Illusions

of

Murder

ISBN: 9798864543313

First published 2023 by Follow This Publishing, Yorkshire (UK)
Text © 2023 Chris Turnbull
Cover Design © 2023 Joseph Hunt of Incredibook Design
Editor: Karen Sanders Editing

For Helen, Mike & Richard
Joy & Jim

To Rosie

Happy Reading!

Turnbull
2023.

ALSO BY CHRIS TURNBULL

The Vintage Coat
Charlie
Carousel

D: Darkest Beginnings
D: Whitby's Darkest Secret
D: Revenge Hits London

It's Beginning To Look A Lot Like Christmas
A Home For Emy
Emy Gets A Sister
Olly The Jack children's series

The Detective Matthews series
Starting with:
The Planting of the Penny Hedge

A Detective Matthews Novel

-3-

Illusions

Of

Murder

Chris Turnbull

"The secret of showmanship consists not of what you really do, but what the mystery-loving public thinks you do."

— **Harry Houdini**

PROLOGUE

FRIDAY 25TH NOVEMBER 1892 - WHITBY

The crowd erupted into rapturous applause.

'Thank you, thank you.' Victor Crown revelled in admiration, his tight, thin lips looking closer to a smirk. He allowed the crowd to go for as long as possible as he lapped up the attention from the centre of the stage. Once the cheering had finally ceased, he began to speak again. 'For my next trick, I require a volunteer from the audience.'

Hands from around the auditorium flew into the air, and the crowd erupted again into pleas and calls for the illusionist's attention. Some volunteered themselves, others pointed over enthusiastically at their friends and relatives. With the house lights raised, the theatre exuded an opulent grandeur, with plush velvet seats, ornate gilded mouldings, and a rich tapestry of red and gold hues that created an atmosphere of timeless elegance.

Victor Crown, dressed in his best long tails suit and bowtie, scanned the audience. He was forty-eight years old, with short, dark, greying hair, and a beard to match. The smile on his face showed how delighted he was by the admiration he received. He had a long, crooked nose, and large round eyes that looked almost grey, with noticeable shadows underneath as though he hadn't slept in years. This was the opening night of his week-long run in Whitby. His show, which had been travelling all around the United Kingdom for the past year, had sold out in Whitby in record time. Having performed for the likes of Queen Victoria and even the President of America, Victor was a well-known figure throughout society.

'You there.' Victor pointed to a lady sitting in the second row. 'Please follow Alice up onto the stage.' Alice was his assistant. A pretty twenty-five-year-old woman with pale skin, engaging crystal blue eyes, and striking ginger hair. Wearing laced boots and a long black and white striped dress, she held out her gloved hand to the volunteer and led her up onto the stage.

The audience fell back into silence as the woman was presented to Victor. Before saying anything to her, he took her hand, looked at it, and stroked his finger across her flat palm. The woman blushed.

'What is your name?' Victor asked quietly, now looking into her eyes.

'Bess…' she stuttered, visibly excited by his presence. 'Beatrice Young.' She was petite, and at twenty-seven, would often be mistaken for a woman much younger. She had mousy brown hair that was tied up and wore a deep purple floor-length dress.

'Who are you here with this evening?'

'My husband, Timothy.'

Victor let go of her hand and turned back to face the audience. Looking back at the spot Beatrice had been sitting, he could see a gentleman with a sobering expression on his face, a furrowed brow, and intensely wide eyes, etched with lines of concern. Victor guessed this must have been her husband. At the side of the stage, Alice was pushing on a large cupboard-type object decorated with gold stars.

'Ladies and gentlemen,' Victor spoke, 'I have selected Beatrice here to assist me in my next trick. Beatrice, can you confirm that we have never met and that you have no idea what is about to happen?'

'Yes,' she shouted, unsure how loudly she needed to speak to be heard at the back.

'I hope your husband doesn't mind, but I am now going to make you vanish from this stage.' The audience sniggered.

Bess looked down at her husband, who was looking anything but amused. He hadn't wanted to attend the show in the first place and was now mortified his wife had become part of the act. He sank lower in his chair and hoped there was nobody else who knew him there.

'Beatrice, please can you enter the vanishing cabinet?' Victor asked as he led her over to the mysterious cupboard. Alice opened the cabinet door and held out her hand for Beatrice, guiding her in and closing the door behind her. The door was closed, and Alice began to spin the cabinet so Victor could bang on each side, proving it was solid.

Beatrice could hear everything from inside the cabinet, and as the cabinet spun, the back compartment split into two and pushed her around into a tight corner. With very little room to move and the temperature rather warm and stuffy, Beatrice still found the whole thing entertaining and continued to listen to Victor talking to the crowd.

'As you can see, ladies and gentlemen, there is no exiting from the back. So, now I tell Beatrice to disappear.' He slapped his hand on the front of the cabinet, making Beatrice jump. Alice then opened the door as wide as possible and, from inside, Beatrice could hear the gasps from the audience. 'Voilà!' shouted Victor and proceeded to knock on the inside walls of the cabinet to showcase them as solid. Beatrice could hear the audience's applause and gasps; she found it thrilling knowing the truth of her disappearance.

Alice then closed the cabinet door and the entire thing was spun again.

'Now is the time to bring her back.' Victor proclaimed to the audience. 'I'm sure her husband would like his beautiful wife returned to him.'

The audience continued to stir. As the cabinet spun again, Beatrice was again pushed by the moving wall back into the centre of the cabinet. The second it stopped, the door was thrust open and Victor grabbed her by the hand and pulled her out onto the stage for a euphoric applause. Beatrice Young emerged, the sudden brilliance of the spotlights momentarily searing her vision as she stepped into the limelight.

Victor allowed Beatrice to take a bow alongside him, and then quickly ushered her off stage so he could soak up the remainder of the applause himself. She returned to her seat full of smiles, though, upon seeing her husband's displeasure, quickly removed the thrilled look from her face.

'Did you enjoy watching that?' she asked him, while the crowd was still applauding. Her husband shrugged. 'Want me to tell you how he did it?'

'Not particularly.' He sighed. 'Is this thing nearly finished?'

'Probably not far off now.'

'Good.' Timothy groaned. Timothy Young was a man of average height, with a slightly hunched posture that seemed to reflect the weight of his troubles. His thinning hair was a shade of dusty brown, combed meticulously to one side in a failed attempt to mask the signs of aging. Deep lines etched his forehead and framed his tired brown eyes, aging him more than his twenty-nine years. They held a mix of weariness and anxiety. His attire, while once respectable, had now taken on a worn and frayed appearance.

Victor Crown and his assistant Alice Grey performed one last trick before the show was completed. For the final trick, Victor made Alice levitate in the centre of the stage, which drew gasps and stunned reactions from the crowd. During his final applause, Victor returned to the stage four times, lapping up the standing ovation he received.

The show was finally over, and the audience began to descend into the dark streets of Whitby. Beatrice couldn't contain the smile on her face and kept thinking about what had happened that evening. As she and her husband walked through the theatre doors onto the street, it began to rain. Small droplets to begin with, but Bess knew it was likely to get heavier.

'I'll get you a cab home so you don't get wet,'

Timothy told her.

'Where are you going?'

'Pub.' He grunted. 'Need it after that.'

'But it's late. Don't you want to come home with me?'

'I'll be home later.' Timothy tried to catch the attention of a passing carriage driver, but he wasn't seen as the horses and cart raced past him.

'I don't need a carriage,' Bess proclaimed. 'It's only a short walk. Anyway, I was hoping we could go to the stage door to try and see Victor as he leaves.'

'It's late. You should go straight home.'

'No, you should come with me.' Beatrice rarely raised her voice, but she was beginning to get irritated at her husband of four years, the strain of their marriage no longer contained behind closed doors. Timothy grimaced at her outburst, but he stayed silent given the number of people still around.

'Absolutely not.' Timothy tutted. 'Are you stupid, woman? Just get in a carriage and go home.'

'No.' Beatrice folded her arms.

'I'm going for a drink,' he repeated quietly. 'I'll

see you later.' He marched off along the street purposefully in the opposite direction to their home.

***

Midnight was fast approaching, and a young woman was walking home after a long night. The rain was much harder now, yet she had no choice but to get wet. As she walked down a set of stairs leading towards the Khyber Pass, her steps were cautious so as not to slip on the cobbles, a mix of fear and determination propelling her forward.

The young woman crossed the Khyber Pass road and walked through a small tunnel cut out of the Cliffside. Reaching the end of the tunnel and still in her own thoughts, she tripped over something in the darkness. She caught herself before landing on the ground, then turned to see what had caught her foot, gasping in horror. There lay the lifeless body of a woman on the floor, her legs at the entrance of the tunnel causing her to trip.

A knot tightened in the young woman's stomach as a cold realization set in—she had stumbled upon a tragedy. Cautiously, she approached the body, struggling to make out the lifeless figure in the darkness. Panic welled up within her, intertwining with a sense of guilt for not seeing the woman in time to avoid tripping over her.

With trepidation, she crouched beside the prone figure, her gloved hand trembling as she reached out to touch the woman's shoulder. She was met with a coldness upon her fingertips, sending a shiver down her spine. Her breath caught as her fingers brushed against the fabric of the woman's dress, now soaked from the heavy rain.

'Hello?' she called and leaned in for a closer look. 'Can you hear me?' She pushed the woman by the shoulder, rolling her onto her back.

The woman was soaked to the bone. She could tell the lifeless woman wasn't breathing now. Her own vulnerability crossed her mind. The alleyway seemed to close in around her, its dark secrets echoing the sombre truth before her.

'Help,' she shouted. 'Is anybody there?' Her words echoed back through the narrow tunnel.

CHAPTER 1

FRIDAY 25TH NOVEMBER 1892

'Is it not time you got home?' Jack taunted Matthews, drinking the last dregs of his pint of beer. 'You never stay out this late, old man.' He slapped his friend on the arm and howled with laughter.

'Grace left this morning for Ripon with Harvey.' Matthews sighed.

'Another attempt to find his brother?'

'Yes.' Matthews drained his glass before continuing. The bar was busy, despite midnight fast approaching. They had managed to get themselves a small table in the corner, though the smoky room gave them very little view of the rest of the bar.

The two men had been sitting inside The Golden Lion pub for several hours, yet it had felt like no time at all. Inside the small, narrow, smoke-filled Victorian pub, dimly lit lanterns cast a warm amber glow that danced upon the worn wooden tables and the weathered faces of patrons huddled in close conversation. The air was thick with the tang of tobacco and the murmurs of shared secrets. A small open fire in the corner kept everyone warm from the chill of the November rain.

'You remember they went looking for him at the workhouse in Thirsk?' said Matthews.

'Yes. Wasn't that months ago?' replied Jack.

'It was. Well, the people at the workhouse gave Harvey an address in Harrogate, but George had apparently left there and started employment somewhere in Ripon. The Ripon address was incorrect, and so the trail went cold.' Matthews shook his head, his tone more defeated than usual. 'Then, just last week, we had word that he was working as a gardener on a manor house estate just north of Ripon. Harvey sent a letter, but nothing came back, and so yet again, he and Grace have headed off in search of him.'

'You don't seem happy about this.'

'I hope he finds George, I really do, but…'

'You're worried he'll be disappointed.' Jack knew Matthews only too well, and his friend's lack of response told him he was correct.

'Anyway, you were supposed to be telling me how the new job's going.' Jack's keen intuition detected Matthews' deliberate shift in conversation, a subtle manoeuvre that did not escape his perceptive gaze.

'It's going great, actually,' Jack replied with a smile. 'The pay's not bad, and I've been learning a lot. I'm feeling good about it.' Jack was one of Matthews' oldest friends, and despite losing touch for some time, they had reconnected a couple of years ago when Matthews returned to Whitby. Jack, an ex-navy officer, looked much older than his twenty-five years with his lined face, large, bushy beard, and dark shaggy hair which was poking out from under his fisherman's beanie. Despite the bar being warm, he was still wearing his thick woollen turtleneck.

'Strange being back on ships?'

'Nah. The navy feels like a long time ago now, and this is completely different, being involved with the building of ships.'

Matthews nodded, happy to hear that his friend was doing well. Detective Benjamin Matthews could not have appeared any more different from his friend if he tried. He was slimmer and taller with a clean-shaven face and short brown slicked-back hair. His green eyes were usually the first thing people noticed about him as they seemed to stand out against the grey backdrop of the town. Matthews was always dressed immaculately, with a clean crisp shirt and waistcoat every day.

They spent the next few minutes speculating whether or not Harvey, who was Matthews' young assistant, would be successful on his latest quest to find his long-lost brother.

'Grand,' Jack said out of the blue, 'but I think I might need another pint before we change the subject.' He stood, grabbed both of the empty glasses on the table, and strode to the bar. Matthews noticed Jack's usual humorous tone had turned stern, and there was a seriousness to his expression that Matthews hadn't seen in a long time.

'Is everything okay?' Matthews asked his friend.

'Of course. We just need more drinks!' he

shouted back while trying to squeeze his way through a cluster of people.

In truth, Jack was nervous. He was trying to get up the courage to tell his friend that his wife, Beth, was pregnant with their first child. Although normally happy news, he knew Matthews and Grace were still struggling to come to terms with their miscarriage only a couple of months ago, and he didn't want to seem insensitive to their feelings. He reached the bar and played over the words he would use in his mind.

Matthews, still at the small corner table, took out his pocket watch. It was a couple of minutes to midnight already. He hoped Grace and Harvey had reached the inn for the night without any issues. They were due to arrive at the manor house the next day.

Jack arrived back at the table, prepared to change the subject, when Matthews reached into his satchel and pulled out a newspaper, which he swiftly thrust under his friend's nose. He pointed to an article in the paper.

'Hey, did you see this?' Matthews asked, his finger tapping on the article.

Jack sighed and took the paper from Matthews' outstretched hand. He recognised the by-line of Miss Clara Blackwell, a young female reporter and a recent addition to the staff at the Whitby Gazette newspaper.

'More negative press,' Matthews muttered as he scanned the article. 'What's her problem with me?'

'Is she claiming you only have the job because of your father again?' Jack asked while scanning the page, his voice laced with annoyance. 'And that your last case was a disaster? What proof does she have on that front?'

Matthews scowled at the article, a knot of anger forming in his stomach. He knew he had earned his position through years of hard work and dedication. He had always tried to do the right thing, even when it was difficult, and he had always taken his duties as a detective seriously.

'She's just trying to stir up trouble,' Jack said, tossing the paper back onto the table. 'I don't know what her deal is, but don't let it get to you.'

Matthews leaned forward, his gaze intent. 'I can't just ignore this. I need to do something about it. Otherwise, people are going to start thinking she's right.'

Jack nodded, his jaw set. He knew Matthews couldn't just sit back and let this reporter's baseless accusations go unchecked. He needed to set the record straight and make it clear that he was a capable detective, regardless of his father's position.

Jack, taking a deep breath, was about to change the subject back to his own news, when they were interrupted by a young boy who approached their table with a sense of urgency. Matthews had spotted the young lad come into the bar only moments before, asking people by the door questions before being pointed in their direction. Matthews tensed as he recognised the look on the boy's face—it was the look of someone who had seen something they shouldn't have.

'Excuse me, sir,' the boy said, addressing Matthews. 'Are you Detective Matthews?' The young boy trembled. Clearly no older than nine, his tattered clothes were a testament to a life of hardship and desperation. He was filthy, and despite the bitter night, was barely wearing anything to help keep away the chill. His bare feet were red and looked sore.

Matthews nodded.

'Finally.' He exhaled, his face breaking into a relieved smile as the weight of his burdens seemed to lift from his shoulders. 'We've been looking for you all over the place.'

'We?' Matthews queried.

'Me and my family, sir.' The young boy took a deep breath before continuing. 'Me ma told us to find you, and only you. Said Detective Matthews had to be the one to know.'

'Know what?' Matthews raised his voice slightly, instantly regretting letting his annoyance come out on this innocent boy. The boy stuttered a story about how he had been scavenging for food in a nearby alley when he had stumbled across the body of a woman.

'Take me there.' Matthews immediately jumped into action, grabbing his coat and heading out of the pub with Jack close behind. They followed the young boy through the streets towards the small alleyway, close to the Khyber Pass.

The night hung heavy over the narrow alley, shadows conspiring with the flickering gas lamps to create an atmosphere of mystery and unease. A small group of people standing helplessly told Matthews they had arrived at the scene. The detective approached with a determined stride, his senses attuned to every detail in the dimly lit space.

'Make way.' Matthews pushed through the crowd, revealing the body of a young woman, lifeless and soaked to the bone due to all the rain.

'We didn't touch her. We just stood watch until James returned with you,' a young woman called out to the detective. By the look of her clothing, Matthews guessed she was the young boy's mother. Crouching beside the body, Matthews studied the scene with the practiced eye of a detective. He noted the position of the victim, the surroundings, and any possible signs of struggle. The chill in the air seemed to match the cold reality of the situation—a life had been extinguished, leaving only questions and a haunting emptiness. He could hear the small group of people whispering behind him.

'Is there anything we can do?' Jack spoke, causing Matthews to momentarily snap out of his thoughts. 'We need to send somebody to the police station to request more assistance. We also need to send for Mr Waters, the coroner.'

'I can head to the station now,' Jack volunteered.

'Good.' Matthews stood and gave his friend a grateful pat on the shoulder. 'They will send word to the coroner. I will stay here and wait with the body.'

'What do you think happened here?' Jack couldn't stop staring at the lifeless woman on the ground.

'It's hard to say right now,' Matthews replied, 'but there was certainly a struggle.'

Jack took his leave and disappeared into the dark night, Matthews returned to checking over the victim but found himself distracted by the people still whispering behind him. Pleased they hadn't left, he questioned them briefly, but as he expected, they had simply stumbled across the body and sent their son in search of Matthews.

'Leave now,' he told them, before thanking them for their help. 'There is nothing more you can do.'

CHAPTER 2

Detective Matthews arrived at Whitby Police Station so early on Saturday morning that sunrise was still hours away. He had not gone to bed at all the night before after learning of the body of the as yet unidentified woman. He had escorted her to the coroner's office before returning home only briefly to freshen up and change.

As he approached the station, he was surprised to see the silhouette of somebody outside the door. Was somebody waiting for him? He approached cautiously, surprised to find it was Clara Blackwell, the young, ambitious newspaper reporter who had

21

written that horrendous article about him in yesterday's paper.

Clara had become known in town only recently as somebody who was eager to make a name for herself. Her articles took aim at many highly respected and influential people in town. Her reputation as a meticulous researcher and a skilled writer with a sharp eye for detail and a talent for crafting compelling stories was one of the reasons her name had been rising for the past two months. Despite her youth and relative lack of experience, Clara was determined to prove herself as a serious journalist and was willing to take risks in pursuit of a good story.

At just nineteen, Clara had a petite frame and delicate features. She had soft, wavy brown hair that was parted in the middle, with a low bun. Her eyes, large and bright, were a deep brown that seemed to change depending on the light. She had a small, upturned nose and full lips that were often set in a determined line, and a porcelain complexion free of blemishes. Her skin had a slight glow to it. Clara was always impeccably dressed, favouring tailored suits and blouses with high collars and long sleeves. She carried herself with confidence and grace, and her movements were precise and purposeful. Despite her small stature, Clara had a presence that commanded attention, and despite only being a part of the Whitby Gazette for such a short time, she had developed a reputation as being a force to be reckoned with.

'Good morning, Detective,' Clara said with a sly grin. 'Any news on the body discovered last night?' Matthews sighed, knowing he was going to have to deal with Clara sooner or later. 'I'm afraid I can't discuss an ongoing investigation with the press, Miss Blackwell,' he said firmly.

Clara's smile faded, replaced by a look of irritation. 'Come on, Detective,' she said, crossing her arms over her chest. 'Do you need to go ask Daddy for permission before you can tell me anything?'

Matthews bristled at the continuous insinuation that he was unfit for his job. 'My position was earned, not inherited. You have no right to print lies, and speaking of which, the article you wrote in yesterday's Gazette was an injustice to the poor family that lost their daughter. You should think about those your lies can hurt.'

Clara rolled her eyes. 'Excuses, excuses,' she said dismissively. 'Well, if you change your mind and want to give a statement to the press, you know where to find me.'

With that, Clara turned on her heel and walked away, leaving Matthews seething. He hated the way she always got under his skin, poking and prodding until he lost his cool. But he couldn't deny that she was good at her job—too good sometimes. He made a mental note to keep a closer eye on her, lest she uncover something he didn't want her to.

Taking a deep breath, Matthews stepped through the entrance of the police station and made his way to his office, bracing himself for another long day of investigating.

The hours passed and daylight crept into the office from the large windows behind the detective's desk. The office comprised of a large oak desk and chair, two rocky wooden chairs opposite him, and a large bookcase against the wall that was unorganised and cluttered with a mixture of books, files, and papers. His desk was littered with papers, notepads, and an ashtray overflowing with his cigarette butts.

Matthews sat at his desk, the candles he had lit now unnecessary as the sunlight shone through the windows, highlighting just how long he had been there.

His pencil scratched against the paper as he worked on his report. He was exhausted but knew he still had a lot of work to do before he could finally sleep. His questioning of the homeless family hadn't resulted in any worthwhile information; they had simply discovered the body sometime after she had died, though exactly when the murder had taken place was still uncertain. The victim also had nothing upon her body to help Matthews identify her. He had just finished detailing the crime scene, the shortest report he had ever written, when he heard a knock at his door.

'Come in,' he called out, not looking up from his notes.

The door opened and his father, Chief of Police David Matthews, stepped inside. He looked tired, his normally sharp features softened by worry lines etched around his eyes.

'Good morning, son. I just wanted to stop in and get any updates on the body you found last night,' he said, taking a seat across from his son. He was a tall man, with broad shoulders and a deep, booming voice. To look at them together, you wouldn't know they were father and son, other than them both being tall. The chief had a greying beard that matched his hair.

Benjamin shook his head. 'Not much to go on yet. The body was badly bruised, clear signs of a struggle, but we are yet to identify the victim. She is currently with Mr Waters, who will perform a post-mortem today.'

The chief frowned, running a hand through his hair. 'Keep me posted, son. In the meantime, we've got another case on our hands that I wanted you to be aware of. A man named Timothy Young is downstairs making a statement that his wife is missing.'

Benjamin's interest piqued at the mention of another case. 'Do you think it's connected to the body we found?'

'It's too early to say, but we can't rule anything out. Normally, I would ask one of the constables to take a statement, but given your new case, I want you to speak to Young and find out everything you can. See if there's any connection between his wife and the victim. If needs be, take him to Mr Waters. If it is his wife, then he'll be able to give us an official identification. If the body is not that of his wife, then the force can take his case and leave you with the homicide.'

Matthews nodded, rising from his chair. 'I'm on it.'

As he made his way downstairs, the prospect of a lead this early on filled him with hope that temporarily made him forget about his exhaustion. As he reached the bottom of the stairs, he spotted Timothy Young waiting for him.

'Mr Young?' Matthews approached, hand extended. Timothy stood and shook the detective's hand. His face fell at the sight of Matthews.

'I thought I would be just giving a statement to one of the officers,' Timothy replied, clearly aware of who Matthews was. It was no surprise to Matthews; most people in town knew who he was these days.

'Well, I will be taking your statement this morning, Mr Young.' Matthews frowned. 'If you'd care to follow me.'

Detective Matthews escorted Timothy Young into the interrogation room so they could speak in private. It was a small, windowless room with only a small table and two chairs within. Matthews lit some candles to give them some light before closing the door.

'Can you start by telling me when you last saw your wife, Mr Young?' Matthews asked, opening up his notebook and readying his pencil.

'It was last night,' Timothy replied, his voice heavy with emotion. 'We went to see Victor Crown's show at the theatre. My wife, Bess, was brought up on stage to help with one of the illusions. She was so excited, but when we left the theatre, we got into an argument.'

'Can you tell me more about your argument with your wife?' Matthews asked, trying to read Timothy's expression.

Timothy shrugged nonchalantly. 'It wasn't anything serious. Just a silly disagreement.'

'What was it about?' Matthews probed.

'It was about the trick Victor Crown performed on her last night. My wife was bragging she knew how it was done and wouldn't stop teasing me about it,' Timothy replied.

Matthews narrowed his eyes. 'And how did that make you feel?'

Timothy scoffed. 'Honestly, I didn't care how the bloody trick was done. I got angry and stormed off, leaving her at the stage door. She wanted to meet Victor after the show, and I just wanted to get out of there.'

Matthews made a note in his notebook. 'And that was the last time you saw her?'

'Yes,' Timothy said with a shrug. 'She wanted to meet Victor Crown. I told her it was late and she should go home, but she wouldn't listen.'

'She should go home?' Matthews repeated. 'Were you not going with her?'

'Well…' Timothy stuttered, as he began to take more notice of his words, 'I told her I wanted to go to the pub, you see, and that I wanted to put her in a carriage home.'

'And did you put her in a carriage?'

'No.' Timothy sighed. 'She refused and said she would rather walk home.'

'Then what happened?'

'Well… I… erm.' Timothy shifted uncomfortably

in his chair, his eyes focused on his hands, which were clasped together on the table in front of him. 'I went to the pub,' he said with an air of disappointment.

Matthews made a note of this information in his notebook. 'Did you see anyone suspicious around the theatre or near the stage door?'

Timothy shook his head. 'No. I didn't notice anything out of the ordinary.'

'Mr Young, can you tell me what time you returned home?'

'It was after three this morning.'

'And I presume there are no signs that your wife had returned to the property at all?'

'No.' Timothy continued to look at his hands. Matthews leaned forward, his eyes still fixed on Timothy, who looked up at the sound of the detective leaning in. 'Mr Young, I need to know if there's anything else you're not telling me. Is there anything at all that might be relevant to this case?'

Timothy fidgeted in his seat, avoiding Matthews' gaze. 'No, nothing comes to mind,' he muttered.

Matthews put down his pencil and leaned back in his chair. He rubbed his chin and looked at the man before him, unsure how much of his story he believed.

'Mr Young, late last night, the body of a woman was discovered in an alleyway close to the Khyber Pass. From the information you have given me, there is a chance this could be your wife.' Mr Young's eyes widened. Matthews paused for a moment before continuing. 'I would like to take you over to the coroner to identify the body of the woman brought in last night.' Mr Young's expression fell to dread. For the first time, he appeared to be speechless. 'Let us hope the woman is not your wife,' said the detective as he rose to his feet.

At that moment, there was a knock on the door, and a young constable entered. He walked directly over to Matthews without even looking at Timothy and leaned in to whisper in the detective's ear. 'Detective, a young woman has arrived to see you. Says she needs to speak to you about the body found last night.'

'Is she able to make a statement with you until I return?' Matthews whispered back.

The young constable shook his head. 'She is

refusing to speak to anyone other than you. She says it's important she speaks to you as soon as possible.'

'Very well. Take her up to my office. I'll be up shortly.'

The constable left the room in silence, and Matthews returned his attention to Timothy. 'I'm afraid something has come up.' Matthews gestured for Timothy to follow him out of the door. 'I will get one of the station carriages to take you to Mr Waters, who will be able to assist you with the identification. He will let me know anything from your visit. I have all your details written down, so I will be in touch if I need to speak with you again.'

The detective escorted Timothy out of the building and into one of the small horse and carriages. He watched him cautiously the whole time. He had a feeling they would be seeing each other again soon.

CHAPTER 3

'Detective Matthews, my name is Miss Martha Bell. I need to speak with you,' the woman said, her eyes wide with fear the moment Matthews walked into his office. Her attire was a patchwork of faded fabrics, her threadbare dress hanging loosely over her slight frame, and her worn shawl failing to shield her from the biting cold that gnawed at the edges of her existence. Despite only being in her twenties, the dirt on her hands and face aged her greatly. A shabby-looking head scarf was bound firmly, keeping her hair tightly beneath.

'Of course, Miss Bell. What brings you here this

morning?' he asked as he walked around his desk and dismissed the constable who had been waiting with her.

'I had to talk to you, Detective. It was me who found that body last night,' she said, her voice low and trembling.

Matthews was taken aback. 'You found the body? Why didn't you say anything last night?'

'I didn't want to get involved, but I couldn't just leave her there.' She spoke with bated breath, as though she had gotten there in a hurry. 'I was walking home from the theatre, where I work, and I stumbled across her lying there. I sent that homeless boy to find you,' Martha said, her eyes brimming with tears.

'Take your time Miss Bell, and when you're ready, tell me everything.' Detective Matthews spoke in a soothing, reassuring tone, his gentle words aimed at calming the anxious Martha Bell.

Martha took a deep breath, her chest rising and falling as she braced herself to recount the haunting events that had unfolded the previous night.

With a sense of trepidation, Martha began her narrative, her voice carrying the weight of the secrets she held. 'It was after my shift at the theatre. I was walking home. The streets were nearly empty, save for a few scattered souls hurrying home. I also recall walking past Alice Grey, the assistant of that illusionist, Victor Crown, who appeared to be hurrying back towards the direction of the theatre. I did think it odd her going back to the theatre given the place was being locked up for the night. She wasn't going to escape the downpour there.' She paused, her eyes distant as she recalled the moment that had set her on a path she never could have anticipated. 'My walk home always takes me across the Khyber Pass and through the little tunnel. I walked briskly, as it was bitterly cold outside and the rain was hellish.'

Detective Matthews leaned forward, his gaze intent on Martha as he absorbed every word. 'Go on,' he encouraged gently, a sense of urgency underlying his patience.

Martha nodded, her voice gaining a note of urgency. 'As I ventured farther down the alley, I tripped over something that nearly sent me flying. I was already trying to tread carefully due to the wet ground.' She swallowed hard, the memory of the grisly discovery seared into her mind. 'There, lying on the ground, was the lifeless body of a young woman. I had tripped over her legs. I hadn't seen her because it was so dark out. I felt terrible about it. I didn't mean to kick her.'

Detective Matthews leaned back in his chair, his expression a mix of concern and curiosity. 'Did you recognise the woman?'

Martha sighed, a sombre sadness in her eyes. 'I didn't know her. But her face… it looked familiar to me for some reason, and then I realised it was the woman Victor Crown had on stage during the show. I know I shouldn't have, but I sneaked into the back of the theatre and watched a small part of the show. We never get to watch anything when working in the bar. It was quiet, and I was curious to see what all the fuss was about.' Martha spoke in a hurried flush, all the while looking down at her hands.

'Did you have any interaction with this woman?' Matthews interrupted. 'Did she come into the bar during the interval?'

Martha shook her head. 'One of the stewards told me they had seen her mouthing off outside the theatre about how the trick had been done, and I think it angered a lot of people who didn't wish to know. I'm sure Victor Crown wouldn't be too happy to hear his secrets being shared around by attention-seeking housewife.'

The room fell into a heavy silence, and Martha looked at the quiet detective with a hesitant glare. Detective Matthews, who had been listening to Martha, paused for thought before speaking, which made Martha nervous in the silence. Finally, Matthews' voice cut through the stillness. 'Martha, you've done a brave thing by coming forward with this evidence. Your information could help propel this case forward.'

Martha nodded, her gaze meeting his with a mix of determination and unease. 'I couldn't stay silent, Detective. I was…'

'May I ask,' Matthews interrupted her. 'Why did you not stay with the body? Why did you send the young boy and then leave?'

'I didn't know what to do. I was so scared. I knew I had to do something, but I didn't want to be involved. Shortly after I discovered the body and called for help, a small homeless family appeared in the passage. They agreed to help, and I told them to go and find you. The mother stayed with the body while the rest of the family and I headed off in search of you. The young boy who found you was checking pubs in case you were out drinking, I'm sure he visited a number of them before finding you,' Martha said, her voice barely above a whisper.

'Miss Bell, why did you not return to the scene and tell me all this at the time?'

'I don't know.' Her shoulders dropped as she let out a loud sigh. My head was all over the place. I just wanted to go home.'

Matthews nodded, understanding her fear. 'You've done the right thing coming forward now, but I have to ask... have you any reason to be fearful for your safety?'

Martha nodded, her eyes widening. 'Yes. I got this pushed under my door overnight,' she said, pulling a crumpled piece of paper from her pocket. It was a handwritten note that read: Stay out of this, or you could end up getting hurt.

Matthews took the note from her, his expression grim. 'Miss Bell, I need you to stay here for a little while longer. I'll have someone take you to a safe place until we figure this out.'

Martha looked nervous. 'Thank you, Detective. But I'm sure I will be okay.'

'You have been sent a threatening note, Miss Bell. That puts you in danger.'

'I could stay with one of my relatives.'

Matthews gave her a reassuring smile. 'Miss Bell, I cannot force you to take my help, but I would suggest it for your own safety. I won't let anything happen to you.'

'Thank you, Detective, but I would rather stay with a family member.'

'If you're sure.' Matthews stood and escorted Martha out of his office and down to the station's front door, where he watched her, intrigued, as she headed down the drive.

Walking back inside, Matthews bumped into his father in the corridor. 'You look exhausted,' the chief told him. 'Did you get any sleep last night?'

'No.' Matthews sighed.

'Well, this case will not get solved with you in this state, so go home. Get some rest, and once we have the coroner's report, I will have it sent over.'

'But...'

'No arguments,' the chief interrupted. 'Go home

and you can continue once we have more information.'

Matthews hated taking orders from his father, but on this occasion, he had to agree with him. He was exhausted and wouldn't be any use to the investigation if he didn't stop to rest. He collected his things and made to leave. He wished Harvey had been there to help him. He had certainly become an invaluable assistant these last few months.

Matthews arrived home at his townhouse on East Crescent, his mind still mulling over the information Miss Bell had given him. He hated returning to an empty house and began wondering how Grace was getting on helping young Harvey. He slouched in his armchair, too exhausted to drag himself upstairs to his bedroom. Within seconds of sitting, he found himself already nodding off. His racing mind kept him drifting in and out of sleep. Without warning, there was a knock at his front door that startled him. He jumped to his feet and bolted into the hallway. Opening the door, he was faced with an officer from the station sent to him as a messenger, holding out a telegram for him.

Matthews snatched the envelope, thanked the

officer, and quickly closed the door. Once back in his sitting room, he opened it with a sense of trepidation. It was from Mr Waters, the coroner, who had already performed the post-mortem on the woman's body. The message was short and to the point: Cause of death strangulation. Body identified as Miss Beatrice Young by her husband. Further details to follow."

Matthews stared at the note for a moment and replayed the last few hours over in his mind. Just a few hours ago, he had no idea who this woman was or any potential motives. Now, he knew that Victor Crown, Alice Grey, and Timothy Young had all just flown to the top of his suspect list.

CHAPTER 4

SATURDAY 26TH NOVEMBER 1892

'**W**ake up.' Grace gave Harvey a gentle tap on the shoulder. 'We're here.' Their horse and cart had left the quiet country road and was now making its way up the long driveway of Norton Conyers manor.

'Is this it?' Harvey yawned, rubbing his eyes and looking out of the carriage window. To either side of the carriage were vast lawns that seemed to go on forever. Harvey was a skinny teenager, with brown scruffy hair that always seemed to be windswept, even after combing it, and his eyes gave him a constant tired appearance.

'I believe so.' Grace gave his hand a little squeeze;

she could sense he was nervous. This wasn't the first time they had gone in search of his brother, George, but this time they had been given information that seemed too good to ignore.

Harvey sat up straight and brushed down his trousers and smart shirt that Grace had made especially for him. He had wanted to make a good impression. Grace had also handmade the trouser braces and blazer he was wearing too. She had made many clothes for Harvey these past few months, as he had nothing to his name when they first met, and she found herself enjoying making things for him. At fifteen years old, he now seemed to be outgrowing her outfits faster than she could make them.

It was a cool morning, and the morning dew on the grass gave a twinkle in the late November sun. The manor house, which was coming up ahead, stood with an understated elegance, its small windows and unassuming door blending seamlessly into its surroundings, a testament to its unpretentious charm. It had just two floors and distinctive Dutch-style gables, making its appearance like nothing Grace or Harvey had ever seen before.

They pulled up to the front door of the manor behind another carriage that had also just arrived. As they disembarked, they saw an older lady dressed in an immaculate dress and coat, with a large hat containing pheasant feathers. 'Can I help you?' she called over to them, an expression of confusion about her.

'Oh, yes.' Grace quickly walked up to her, a hand outstretched to greet. Grace was wearing an olive-green gown with a matching hat which neatly sat upon her golden hair that was tied up. Her makeup was always subtle, and despite the early start, she still managed to look fresh and full of smiles as she approached the lady before her.

'Good morning. My name is Grace Matthews, and this is Harvey,' she began. 'We've come from Whitby on a rather unique mission.'

'Lady Graham,' the older woman introduced herself and held out her hand and shook Grace's. 'Well, I must say, you have intrigued me.' Lady Graham's eyes held curiosity as she regarded them. 'A unique mission, you say?' She was wearing a large oversized brown coat and a rain bonnet to protect her immaculate grey hair from any rain. She wore large, thin, high boots that resembled riding boots. Despite being dressed for comfort, she still maintained a full face of makeup, including bright red lipstick.

Grace nodded, her expression earnest. 'Yes. You see, Harvey here has been searching for his long-lost brother, George. We were informed that he might be working here on the estate.'

Lady Graham's features softened, her eyes reflecting empathy. 'Ah, a family reunion. I can understand the significance of such a journey.'

Grace smiled warmly, feeling a sense of kinship with the lady of the house. 'Indeed. It's been a long search, and we're hoping that our efforts will bear fruit here.'

Lady Graham gestured for them to enter, her demeanour welcoming. 'Please, come inside. We shall make inquiries and do our best to assist you in your search.'

As they stepped into the interior of the manor, Grace couldn't help but feel a sense of hope mingling with the anticipation that had brought them to this place. She welcomed them warmly inside and offered them a seat by a large open fireplace to warm up. Lady Graham also requested hot drinks and food from the butler, as she could see that they were both exhausted.

The formal sitting room they found themselves in exuded an air of timeless elegance, its walls adorned with intricate floral wallpaper and paintings that Grace and Harvey guessed were of previous owners and family members. The polished hardwood floors adorned with plush Persian rugs conjured an atmosphere of sophistication, where elegant gatherings and hushed conversations seemed to be held in high regard. Grace and Harvey seated themselves on a large sofa that sank them into it as they sat.

'Now then.' She sat in a large armchair opposite them. 'How can I help you?'

'His name is George Allen,' Grace continued, looking at Harvey, who seemed more than happy for Grace to take the lead.

'Allen, you say.' Lady Graham furrowed her brow and tapped a finger against her lips, her expression tinged with puzzlement as she strained to recall the name she had just been told. 'I'm afraid I don't know of any George Allen working here,' she said apologetically.

Grace and Harvey exchanged a worried look. They had come so far, but now it seemed their journey was again in vain.

'But not to worry. I'm often forgetful when it comes to names. I can send word to the groundskeeper and find out if he knows of a George Allen.' Harvey's face fell, and disappointment clouded his features as he absorbed the possibility of again reaching a dead-end trail.

When the butler returned with drinks and food, Lady Graham requested he send a message to the groundskeeper. Harvey tucked into the pastries on the table in front of them.

'Have you had the pleasure of visiting this area before?' Lady Graham asked as she sipped on her cup of tea.

'No. This is the first time for us both,' Grace replied, a large smile on her face in gratitude for the gracious hospitality they were receiving.

'Did you know Charlotte Bronte visited this house once?' she asked them with excitement.

'Oh, I adore her books.' Grace beamed.

'Of course, that was a long time ago,' Lady

Graham continued. 'Though, I confess I wish I had been alive at the time to have met her.'

The conversations between Grace and Lady Graham flowed so well that they hadn't realised any time had passed at all when the butler returned with another man; it was the groundsman.

'Ah, Mr Barnes. There you are.' Lady Graham beamed at the sight of him. She retold Harvey's story to the groundsman about how she was trying to help him find his brother. Mr Barnes listened carefully to Harvey's story and then thought for a moment.

'We have a couple of new lads working on the grounds these last few months,' he said finally. 'There's a young man who can usually be found working in the garden. I don't recall his surname, but I'm certain he's called George.'

Harvey's face lit up with hope, and Grace couldn't help but smile at his enthusiasm.

'Where can we find him?' Grace asked eagerly.

Mr Barnes scratched his chin thoughtfully. 'I'm not sure if he's around now, but I can go and look for him. It might take a while, though.'

Grace and Harvey agreed to wait, and Mr Barnes

left to search for George.

As they waited, Lady Graham offered them a bed for the night. 'You couldn't possibly travel all the way back to Whitby today,' she insisted. 'I'll have some rooms made up for the both of you.'

'Thank you, Lady Graham.' Grace was humbled and too exhausted to refuse her invitation.

Finally, after what seemed like hours, Mr Barnes returned, leading a young man towards them.

'This young man says his name is George,' he told them, gesturing towards the man beside him. He was a tall and lean fellow in his early twenties, with sharp and angular features. He had a strong jawline and piercing brown, sleepy eyes set deep in their sockets, a tiredness about them that almost mirrored those of Harvey's. His hair was dark and tousled, falling in waves to his shoulders. He wore a rough-looking jacket with holes in it over a simple white shirt that was old and greying, and dark trousers. Despite his somewhat dishevelled appearance, George carried himself with an easy confidence and seemed to have a certain charisma, his face puzzled as to why he had been brought into the main house.

'I will leave you now,' said Mr Barnes, as he

backed out of the room.

'I too will give you some privacy.' Lady Graham hurried out of the room after Mr Barnes.

'Is there something I can help you with?' George asked, a clear expression of confusion as he looked upon the two unfamiliar faces before him. Grace hesitated. She wanted to give Harvey the opportunity to speak first, but for some reason, he had frozen.

'Please, take a seat,' Grace finally offered George. 'We simply wish to speak with you.'

Harvey couldn't believe his eyes as he finally lay them on his older brother; his heart was pounding in his chest. It had felt like such a long time, and yet now there he was in the same room.

'George, this is my friend, Mrs Grace Matthews. She has been helping me look for you,' Harvey said, his voice shaking with emotion. 'I'm Harvey. Harvey Allen. Your little brother.'

George regarded Harvey with a mixture of confusion and disbelief, his eyes locked onto his younger brother as if trying to comprehend what he had just heard. He then looked between Lady Graham and Grace, his face flushed pink with embarrassment at them staring at him. 'I don't have a little brother,' he said coldly. 'You must have the wrong person.'

Harvey's face fell. He had been so sure George would be happy to see him and learn he had a family. 'I'd been living with our grandmother in Whitby, and when she died only a couple of months ago, I discovered papers in her possession about you. It said you had been in the workhouse, and we've been trying to find you ever since.'

George's expression darkened at the mention of the workhouse. 'I left that place behind me for good. I never want to have to think about it again,' he said. Turning away from Harvey, he made to leave.

'Wait,' Grace and Harvey called out in unison. George stopped in his tracks and spoke without turning around. 'What is it you want from me?'

'I… I…' Harvey was speechless; this was not how he had pictured meeting his brother would go.

'Harvey was simply trying to find you,' Grace interjected. 'He has no family left in his life and, upon discovering he has a brother, he was hoping to find you and have some kind of relationship with you.'

George's face returned to looking at Grace and Harvey. It was clear that he was overwhelmed with this sudden revelation. 'I have no intention of ever returning to Whitby. I've done my time there, and I have no desire to be reminded of it. You're nothing but a stranger to me.'

Tears pricked at Harvey's eyes. He couldn't believe his brother didn't want anything to do with him. 'Please, George. I can offer you a place to stay, a family. We can start a new life together as real brothers.'

'I'm sorry, but we're not brothers. Maybe in blood, but nothing else. My mother left me to the workhouse. I'm not sure I can forgive her. Whitby has nothing but bad memories for me now. I want to move on.' George turned and began to leave again.

A lump formed in Harvey's throat. He had always hoped he would find his brother and they could be reunited. But it seemed George had moved on from his past and had no interest in reconnecting with his family.

'I understand,' Harvey said, his voice barely above

a whisper as he watched his brother head for the door. 'I won't bother you again, George. I just wanted to see you and make sure that you were okay.'

George glanced back at Harvey, his expression softening slightly. 'I appreciate your concern, but I don't need anyone looking out for me. I'm fine on my own.' And with that, he walked out of the room. Harvey watched as his brother left. Tears welled up in his eyes as a profound sense of sadness and disappointment washed over him, weighing heavily on his heart. He had found his brother, but it seemed their reunion was not meant to be.

CHAPTER 5

SATURDAY 26TH NOVEMBER 1892

Evening was fast approaching, and Matthews decided it was time to pay a visit to Victor Crown. He knew Victor was scheduled to be on stage again that night, so he knew exactly where he was going to be.

The November evenings were drawing in fast, and it had been dark outside for a few hours already by the time Matthews left his office for the theatre.

Matthews stood before the grand entrance, where a growing crowd had gathered in anticipation of the night's performance. He had no time for queues and pleasantries, his focus solely on the enigma that was Victor Crown and the secrets that seemed to entwine themselves around the illusionist's world.

Casting a determined glance at the ornate entrance, Matthews turned his steps towards the stage door at the side of the building. He reached out, knocking with a sense of purpose that conveyed his urgency. The door opened slowly, revealing an usher, who regarded him with a mixture of reluctance and curiosity.

'Can I help you?' the young boy asked hesitantly.

'Detective Matthews. I require entry.'

'Detective Matthews.' The usher's voice was laced with wariness. 'What brings you here tonight?'

'I've come to speak with Mr Crown and his associates,' Matthews replied firmly, his gaze fixed on the usher's eyes.

The usher hesitated, seemingly torn between duty and scepticism. Finally, he stepped aside, allowing Matthews to step into the narrow, grimy corridor which stretched on ahead, its dim lighting barely penetrating the layers of dirt and cobwebs that clung to the walls, and a musty smell of damp timber, a real contrast to the glitz and glamour of the public facade.

As he made his way towards the heart of the

theatre, Matthews couldn't help but feel a sense of unease settling around him. The air was heavy with anticipation.

The corridor behind the stage door was deserted other than the usher who had granted him entry. 'Where is Mr Crown?'

'He'll be in his dressing room,' the young lad replied, shifting uneasily from foot to foot and fidgeting with his hands, his discomfort palpable. 'He'll be going on stage soon, though, so he won't want to be disturbed.'

'Noted.' Matthews thanked the lad and marched off along the corridor in the direction he was pointed. He could hear the audience talking and shuffling around in the auditorium, though he couldn't see the stage.

As he crept along the dimly lit corridors, he could hear the muffled sounds of angry voices coming from one of the dressing rooms. Matthews frowned, wondering what they were arguing about. He moved closer to the door to try and hear more.

Inside, he could hear two men. One of them he guessed to be that of Victor Crown, the star of the show. The other voice was unfamiliar, but Matthews guessed from the way they were speaking that he was Victor's manager.

'I told you, I won't do it!' Victor Crown's voice was loud and angry.

'Victor, I'm telling you, we can't afford to have any more incidents like last night. You are booked up for months. If something were to happen, we would both be ruined,' his manager replied.

'I don't see what the problem is.' Victor's tone was defensive. 'Nothing can be proven to connect my show.'

'Someone was killed, Victor. Do you realise what kind of trouble we could be in if the police link this to you and the show?'

'They're not going to find out,' Victor said confidently. 'We've got everything under control. Nobody could have predicted what happened. It was an unrelated accident.'

'But what about that journalist, Miss Blackwell?' his manager asked. 'She's already been poking around, asking questions.'

Victor sneered. 'What does she know? She's just a busybody.'

'She knows enough to be dangerous. She's

threatening to run with a story about your past relationships and misdemeanours. We can't afford any negative press.'

'What are you suggesting?' Victor asked, his tone suspicious.

'I've already told you, we need to take care of her,' his manager said, his voice low and ominous. 'Permanently.'

Detective Matthews couldn't believe what he was hearing. However, he knew better than to jump to conclusions and needed to make sure he had the facts before jumping in. Matthews heard footsteps approaching the door and quickly retreated into the shadows. The door opened and the manager emerged, closing the door behind him and mumbling to himself with annoyance.

Matthews followed the manager into the dimly lit bar, his footsteps echoing on the hardwood floor. The small bar was packed with patrons enjoying drinks before the show, making it difficult for Matthews to pick out his suspect.

Finally, he spotted the man he was looking for—a tall, thin man with slicked-back hair and a nervous expression. Matthews made his way over.

'My name is Detective Matthews,' he said. 'I need to ask you a few questions about the murder that took place last night.'

'Excuse me?' The gentleman's face registered a startled surprise as he looked up at the detective, his features momentarily frozen in astonishment.

'You are the manager of Victor Crown, are you not?'

'Yes.' The man looked Matthews up and down before continuing. 'Harry Denton.' He held out his hand to shake the detective's.

'I'm sure you will have heard about the incident that took place last night,' Matthews said. 'It involved a lady who attended last night's performance.'

Harry Denton's expression grew serious as he set down his glass. 'Of course. Gossip always travels fast in small towns like this, even to those of us just visiting.'

At that moment, a steward announced in the doorway that the performance was about to begin, and the crowded bar quickly emptied, leaving the two men to talk in private.

'When did you and Victor arrive in town?' asked

Matthews.

'Victor usually arrives the day before a performance. I always arrive a few days before him to ensure everything is ready for his arrival. I travel with most of the equipment and personally see that it arrives at the theatre safely.'

'Have you been to Whitby before?'

'This is our first time bringing a show here.'

'Did you know the woman who died?' Matthews asked.

Harry shook his head. 'No, I didn't. But I heard that she was at the opening night of our show.'

Matthews leaned in. 'Do you have any reason to believe Victor Crown or anybody associated with this company might have been involved in some way?'

A look of genuine surprise painted Harry Denton's face. 'Why would you think that?'

'Mr Crown is not exactly squeaky clean when it comes to the law,' Matthews said. 'I know Miss Clara Blackwell is working on a tell-all article about some of his shadier past.' Matthews was bluffing. He'd had no idea about that until he overheard Victor and his manager talking about it just minutes ago, but he was hoping his bluff would pay off.

The manager looked thoughtful for a moment. 'I don't know about any shady past, but I do know Victor has been under a lot of stress lately. We've had some financial difficulties with the show, and I think he's been feeling the pressure.'

'Is that why you and Victor were arguing backstage a short time ago? Care to explain what that was about?'

Harry Denton's face dropped at the realisation they had been overheard. He hesitated for a moment before responding. 'It was just a disagreement over money,' he said. 'Victor's been having some financial troubles lately, as I mentioned. We tend to disagree when it comes to these things and Victor can get somewhat... passionate with his response.'

'Interesting,' Matthews retained a perfect poker face, 'for you see I could have sworn it was not money I heard you arguing over, but it did sound like you were discussing my case.' Harry's eyes widened. 'Doors are not the best soundproofing when it comes to private conversations, Mr Denton.' Matthews saw Harry gulp as his brow became glazed with sweat. 'Now, what about Victor's assistant, Alice Grey?'

The manager's face turned sour at the mention of her name. 'What about her?'

'She is just one of many people I will require speaking to in this investigation.' Matthews remained composed as he watched Harry Denton look more and more uncomfortable.

'Alice is a troublemaker, always causing drama. Victor has been spending a lot of time with her lately, trying to teach her new illusions for the show, to be more involved. I think he sees her as a protégé of sorts.'

'I have reason to believe that Miss Grey was close to the scene of the crime shortly before the body was discovered. Do you think this is suspicious?' Matthews raised an eyebrow.

'Pardon?' Confusion clouded Harry Denton's face as he was confronted with the question, leaving him momentarily at a loss for words.

'Do you know why she would be around that area so late at night?' Matthews expanded his question.

Harry sighed, clearly becoming bored of the conversation. 'She's been taking up Victor's time and attention for a while now instead of letting him focus on the show, and she knows how to manipulate him. I don't know why she would be in the area so late. I'd have expected her to be in Victor's bed if I'm honest. But if you're implying what I think you are, then the answer is no, I don't think she's capable of murder.'

'I will require to speak to Mr Crown and Miss Grey, ideally after the show this evening.'

The manager looked down at his shoes, clearly uncomfortable. 'Look, Detective,' he said finally. 'I don't know anything about the murder. All I know is that we need to put on a good show tonight and for the remainder of the week. We can't afford any bad press. You understand?'

'I understand,' he said, 'but I need you to be honest with me. Is there anything else you can tell me that might help me solve this case?' Matthews couldn't get a handle of his man, during their interactions. He couldn't help but wrestle with conflicting thoughts. On one hand, Harry had an air of sophistication and charisma that made it easy to believe he had no knowledge regarding the case at all. His demeanour was persuasive, and he seemed genuinely shocked by the unfolding events. Yet, beneath the surface, Matthews couldn't ignore the subtle inconsistencies in Harry's behaviour. There were moments when Harry appeared guarded, as if he were holding back information, but could this simply be him protecting his client? After all, that was what he was being paid for.

'I will tell you if I hear anything,' He stretched out his hand to shake the detective's again before excusing himself.

Matthews remained in the bar where he took out his notepad and began to scribble down his thoughts while they were fresh in his mind.

With the sound of the show in full swing, Detective Matthews entered the theatre's deserted grand foyer, the ornate architecture and lavish decorations contrasting sharply with the air of tension that seemed to linger in the space. He made his way to the manager's office, where Mr Thomas Archer, the beleaguered theatre manager, waited.

As Matthews entered the room, Mr Archer looked up from his desk, his expression a mixture of exhaustion and frustration. 'Ah, Detective Matthews. It's good to see you. I thought I might see you today.' His voice carried an undertone of strain.

Matthews nodded, taking a seat opposite the manager. 'Mr Archer, I've been conducting inquiries related to my current investigation. I'd like to ask you a few questions about Victor Crown and his manager, Harry Denton.'

Mr Archer let out a sigh as if relieved to finally have an outlet for his grievances. 'Detective, I'll be frank with you. Victor Crown and Harry Denton have proven to be nothing short of a challenge since they arrived here. Demanding, temperamental. Their presence has been a constant source of stress.'

Matthews leaned forward, his expression attentive. 'Could you elaborate on their behaviour?'

The theatre manager's gaze turned sombre. 'It's been an ongoing series of disagreements and clashes. Victor is meticulous about his performances, often insisting on last-minute changes and adjustments that disrupt the entire schedule. Harry, on the other hand, handles the business affairs, but his demeanour is far from accommodating.'

Matthews raised an eyebrow. 'Can you provide

examples?'

Mr Archer sighed, running a hand through his hair. 'Just yesterday, they had a heated argument right in the middle of the lobby, loud enough for all the staff to hear. It's clear they don't see eye to eye on many matters. It was shortly before the doors opened on opening night.'

'Have their disagreements escalated to anything more serious?' Matthews inquired, his instincts urging him to probe further.

The manager hesitated before answering. 'There have been rumours of threats exchanged. Veiled accusations that hint at deeper conflicts. But as far as I know, it's mostly been verbal clashes.'

Matthews nodded, his thoughts racing. The puzzle seemed to be getting more intricate by the minute. 'Thank you for your honesty, Mr Archer. May I ask you to keep an eye on them both for me and let me know if you hear or see anything you think I should be aware of.'

'Of course, Detective.' Mr Archer groaned. 'I can't tell you how happy I'll be when this blasted week is over.'

As he left the manager's office, Matthews couldn't

shake the feeling that the animosity between Victor Crown and Harry Denton held more significance than initially apparent.

CHAPTER 6

SATURDAY 26TH NOVEMBER 1892

Matthews spent the next few hours sitting in the theatre bar. He found it strange being able to hear the occasional applause and cheers from the auditorium with no context on what was impressing the audience so much. He, like many others in society, had heard of Victor Crown before, but Matthews couldn't claim to know much about the man other than his headlines that occasionally made the papers. He remembered when this show was announced. It seemed the entire town was in a frenzy about the famed illusionist coming to Whitby; even Grace had talked about it for days.

Matthews took out his pocket watch; it was almost ten o'clock. The evening's performance would be drawing to a close soon. Eager to catch Victor before he left the building, Matthews returned to the backstage area, and to Victor's dressing room, though, this time, he let himself inside. It was completely dark and was a smaller room than Matthews had expected, with no windows.

Using the little light shining through from the corridor, Matthews could see a small dressing table with a mirror, with papers littering the surface, and he approached to take a closer look. The letters appeared to be mostly from fans and admirers; nothing of interest to him. As his eyes began to adjust to the darkened room, he could see there were clothes strewn about, magic props scattered across the table, and a musty smell in the air. He searched through drawers, cabinets, and shelves, looking for anything that could provide a clue to the murder. But as he searched, he found nothing.

He found a single used candle under some papers. He fumbled in his pocket for a matchbox, and once he had lit the candle, Matthews raised it to see more of the room. Shocked by the sight of a face staring back at him through the mirror, Matthews dropped the candle, which extinguished itself as it fell. He stumbled backwards in fright and tripped over a thin wooden chair, landing on the floor.

'I hope you are okay, Detective.' Victor Crown's voice came from the doorway, his face lit by a large candelabra in his hand. 'I should have warned you. I have an automaton in here. Can be quite a shock in the dim light.' He held out a hand and helped Matthews back onto his feet.

The thing Matthews had seen in the mirror was that of an automaton, a mechanical device designed to perform tasks or imitate human actions, often with intricate and lifelike movements.

'Quite all right.' Matthews brushed himself off, though he knew even without looking in the mirror that his face had turned bright red. The automaton was of a young boy, sitting perfectly still on a high stool. The doll had a porcelain face and was dressed in a fancy costume, not dissimilar to a young boy's Sunday best. Its lifelike features were unnerving to say the least. It was intricate, with tiny mechanical parts and gears that made it move.

'I've had him for years. He was supposed to be on stage with me this week, but there seems to be a fault.' Victor placed the large candelabra on the dressing table, covering his fan letters with little concern; the room was already much easier to see in now. 'Did you enjoy the show, Detective?'

'I'm afraid I didn't see the performance.'

'Ah, no matter,' Victor replied. 'We have plenty more performances before we leave. I will have to get you a ticket in the VIP box, you can bring a guest.'

'There is no need,' Matthews replied. 'I am simply here to speak with you about a recent murder in the town.'

'Of course, Detective.' Victor sounded calm and relaxed. 'Do you mind if I change while we talk? This waistcoat is not as loose as it once was. I really should get myself another.' Victor began unbuttoning his red velvet waistcoat before removing the cufflinks from his shirt.

'Mr Crown, you don't seem surprised to see me in your dressing room,' Detective Matthews remarked as he continued to cast a sharp, appraising gaze around the room while Victor changed.

Crown turned from the mirror where he'd been adjusting his collar. His eyes met Matthews', and a sly smile played at the corners of his lips. 'My manager informed me you were in the building and waiting to speak with me.'

Matthews furrowed his brow, a sense of unease settling over him. 'I see. Did he tell you anything else?'

Crown hesitated for a moment, then leaned closer, lowering his voice. 'Yes. He told me that the Glasgow theatre has just confirmed the dates for my show.'

Matthews blinked in surprise, caught off guard by the unexpected turn in the conversation. 'I beg your pardon?'

'You asked me if Harry told me anything else.' Victor smirked. 'That's what he told me.'

'I meant about the investigation.'

'Ah, well then...' Victor removed his shirt and carefully hung it on a temporary hanger before buttoning it back up. 'You should be more specific with your questions.' The illusionist's enigmatic smile seemed to mirror the very essence of the room, as if secrets were hidden in every shadow.

'Mr Crown,' Matthews continued, his tone firm yet laced with curiosity. 'I'd like to discuss the ongoing investigation with you.'

Victor casually picked up a clean shirt that had been lying over the small wooden chair, his concentration focused on the buttons instead of Matthews. 'Investigations, Detective, are much like my performances. Full of intrigue and surprises.'

Matthews narrowed his eyes slightly, his patience tested by Victor's cryptic response. 'I'm looking into the events of last night, particularly the connection between you, your assistant Alice Grey, and the unfortunate victim.'

Victor's gaze seemed to pierce through the detective, his smile widening as if he held secrets too vast to be contained. 'Connections. They often weave intricate patterns that are only discernible to those who truly seek.'

'Mr Crown, I do not have time for your games. We need concrete information," Matthews pressed, his frustration mounting.

Victor straightened, his gaze holding a mixture of amusement and something deeper. 'Ah, Detective, it seems you're determined to unravel the threads of illusion and truth. But remember, in this realm of shadows, appearances can be deceiving.'

The detective's frustration boiled over, his voice sharper now. 'Stop speaking in riddles, Mr Crown. This is a serious matter. You and your assistant are currently suspects in a murder case. I would expect you to be a little more concerned.'

Victor's smile held a touch of wistfulness as he finally met Matthews' gaze directly. 'Detective, beneath the surface of riddles lies a tapestry woven with secrets and revelations. Perhaps, in time, the threads will align. You are just yet to ask the right questions.'

'You have just returned from America, I believe?' Matthews changed tactics.

'Indeed. I often do shows over there. it's also a good place to meet other performers like myself.'

'Do you meet many who perform illusions like you?'

'I've had the honour of meeting many during my time. This last visit to America, I met a young man at Coney Island, who I believe will be well known one day. His name is Erik Weisz, and his passion for learning magic and escapology is something I have not seen in a long time. Coney Island is the perfect place to practise your skill in front of an audience, you know, Detective. It's a real place for misfits.'

'Did you have to train to become a performer? Or are you self-taught?' Matthews sensed himself verging into curiosity rather than getting on with questions related to the case, but it seemed to be making Victor speak in fewer riddles, so he was happy to keep going for now.

'I discovered the love of magic when I was a boy and started to perform to small crowds from the age of thirteen. When I was nineteen, I went to Paris and worked as an apprentice for the French illusionist Jean-Eugène Robert-Houdin. He had retired from performing by this time, but he took me on in his workshop. He had originally been a watchmaker before becoming the well-known performer and had decided to retire from performing and return to his creative routes. He had a workshop for designing and making automatons. He was quite an artist, and his designs were almost as desirable as the finished piece.'

'You speak fondly of this man as though he was

your own father.'

'I spent four years as his apprentice, and I admired him greatly. He taught me everything I needed to become a performer, and I even perform some of his specially created acts.'

'Mr Crown, I need to ask you some questions about the death of Bess Young.'

Victor's face fell, and he looked away. 'Yes, of course. It's a tragedy, Detective.'

'Do you recall her being the woman you brought up on stage to assist with a trick?'

'I wouldn't simply by her name, but I am told that this is who the woman was. I can assure you, Detective, that I had nothing to do with her death,' Victor said, his tone firm.

'I understand that, Mr Crown,' Matthews replied. 'But I need to know if you saw anything or anyone suspicious last night.'

Victor shook his head. 'I'm sorry, Detective. After the show, I usually return to my dressing room where I stay for quite some time before leaving in a carriage for my bed. I usually stay here a while to give the audience time to leave.'

'What time did you leave?'

'It must have been around half past eleven. I was in my room at The White Horse and Griffin ten minutes later.'

'Why are you not staying at The Royal hotel? It's a lot closer.'

'I prefer smaller places, with fewer rooms,' Victor replied while changing into different trousers. 'Smaller places allow me to book up entire floors, meaning I am less likely to be disturbed. A larger hotel has more rooms with the likelihood of fans trying to get to me.'

Matthews nodded and jotted down some notes. 'What about Alice Grey? What time did she leave last night?'

'I don't know. I always request privacy after a show to relax and wind down. I don't usually see Alice until the next morning.'

'So, you're saying you didn't see Alice after the show last night?'

'Briefly. We spoke in my dressing room shortly after curtain, but then I presume she left after that.'

'Is she still around for me to question this evening?'

Victor's expression changed slightly. 'Alice was

given the night off,' he said, his voice slightly strained.

Matthews raised an eyebrow. 'Is that so? May I ask why?'

Victor sighed. 'My manager doesn't like her. He's been pressuring me to fire her for weeks. Then when I heard about the murder this morning, I couldn't handle any more reasons for him to argue with me, so I finally caved and gave her tonight off, just to appease him. Buggers up the bloody show a bit as I rely on her quite a bit, but I've done shows solo before, so I can manage.'

'Why does your manager want you to fire her?'

'He's never liked her. He thinks she's too ambitious, too pushy. He thinks I listen to her more than I listen to him. But I've worked with Alice for years now, and I know she's a hard worker and a great assistant on stage.'

'Do you have any idea where I might find her?'

Victor shook his head. 'I'm afraid not, Detective. She's free to do as she pleases on her nights off. She's a bit of a free spirit, you might say. I haven't seen her at all today. I guess she's unhappy with me for caving into Denton's request and having her not appear on stage tonight. She has a room at the Griffin too, so I can't imagine she'll have gone far.'

Matthews sighed, frustrated. 'All right. I'll keep a look out for her. But in the meantime, if you hear from her or see her before I manage to speak with her, please let me know. It's important that I speak to her as soon as possible.'

'I will,' Victor promised.

As Matthews turned to leave, Victor spoke up again. 'Detective, there's one more thing you should know about Alice. It might not be relevant to your investigation, but I think you should know anyway.' Matthews turned back to face him. 'What is it?'

Victor hesitated again, then spoke in a low voice. 'I met Alice in London many years ago. However, she was born right here in Whitby. She's been a little twitchy in the lead-up to these shows. She never told me what happened, but I get the impression she was happy to get away and start afresh.'

Detective Matthews raised an eyebrow at Victor's statement regarding Alice.

CHAPTER 7

Detective Matthews woke up on Sunday morning to an empty house. He rubbed his eyes and sat up in bed, feeling the weight of the case on his mind. He glanced around the empty bedroom, missing his wife, who was still out of town helping Harvey with his search for his brother. This wasn't the first time that she had gone out of town with Harvey, and each time, they had returned looking more and more disappointed not to have found George. He was hoping this would be the last time.

He had never realised just how quiet his grandmother's old house was until Grace had started leaving to help Harvey.

He got out of bed and walked over to the window, pulling back the curtains to let in the morning light. He paused and gazed out of his bedroom window, the glass framing a tableau of contrasts—a quiet street bathed in the hushed hues of the early morning, juxtaposed against the restless expanse of the choppy North Sea. Dark clouds were drawing in and seagulls filled the sky with their high-pitched wails.

That morning, he was meeting his sister, Charlotte, her husband, John, and his nephew, Hugo at church. He would usually attend with Grace and thought that with her being out of town he'd have been able to get out of it, but his sister had insisted he join them instead, fearful that he was lonely.

Matthews knew he needed a break from the case, at least for a little while. Exhaustion settled heavily upon him, his weary eyes a testament to a night spent meticulously writing notes and poring over them. He needed to clear his head, to focus on something else, and Charlotte was also good at achieving that.

He put on his best suit and tie and made his way to St Hilda's church. He realised he had left the house earlier than necessary; he usually had to wait for Grace to finish getting dressed. Instead of sitting around with his own thoughts, he walked the long way there. Matthews strolled through the streets of Whitby, a temporary respite from the demands of his investigation, finding solace in the tranquil rhythm of the harbour and watching the fishing boats coming in with their morning catch as he whiled away the moments before the call of Sunday church.

Eventually arriving at the church, he waited by the entrance for his sister. He nodded politely to the familiar faces of the townspeople who walked by. The cool breeze of the morning sent shivers down his spine, and he rubbed his hands together for warmth. It had been a couple of weeks since he last saw Charlotte, and he was excited to catch up with her.

Distracted by the sudden influx of people, Matthews eventually spotted his sister approaching him, pushing an enormous pram with her three-month-old baby, Hugo, inside. She greeted him with a smile. 'Good morning, Uncle Benji.' She leaned over to kiss her brother on the cheek.

Charlotte wore a burnt orange dress with a brown shawl around her shoulders to keep her warm. She looked well and put on a brave smile considering Matthews knew how much she was struggling as a new mother.

'Good morning, sis. Good morning, Hugo,' Matthews replied, returning the smile. 'How's my little nephew doing?'

'He's doing well, thank you for asking,' Charlotte said as she lifted the blanket covering Hugo's face so Matthews could see him. The baby was sound asleep, bundled up warm.

'He's grown so much since I last saw him,' Matthews said, looking at the baby with fondness.

'Yes. He just eats and grows.' Charlotte smirked, but behind the smirk, Matthews could tell she was exhausted.

'Are you... erm... getting on okay?' He didn't want to offend her.

'Oh, just tired. Nothing different to any other new mother.'

'No John with you this morning?'

'He's already inside. They asked for some volunteers to help play the organ after Mrs Lambert died last month. John plays the piano, so I put his name forward,' She gave a girl-like giggle. 'He wasn't too happy when I told him, but it's only until they find somebody more permanent.'

Matthews offered to take the pram, as there were a couple of steps to manoeuvre in order to enter the church. Charlotte gladly allowed her brother to take it, as she knew only too well how heavy it was.

Just as they were about to enter the church, Clara Blackwell arrived, and Matthews was momentarily distracted. He was eager to speak with her about the article she was writing on Victor Crown. He had a hunch that she might know something that could help him with his investigation.

'Charlotte, I'm sorry, but I have to speak with Clara for a moment,' Matthews said once he'd got the pram to the top of the steps. 'I'll meet you inside, okay?'

Charlotte nodded and headed inside the church with the pram, and Matthews approached Clara. 'Good morning, Miss Blackwell,' he said with a friendly smile.

'Detective,' Clara acknowledged him as she continued to walk on by. Clara, known for her unconventional style, appeared at church in a deep blue dress that stood in stark contrast to her usual attire, embracing a sense of elegance that hinted at a hidden facet of her persona.

'If I may have a moment of your time, Miss Blackwell.'

Clara stopped in her tracks, her expression clear that she was not in the mood for any kind of argument or disagreement. 'What brings you here?' Clara asked. 'I thought you attended Sunday mass at St Mary's?'

'Usually, I do. However, this week I'm accompanying my sister, and this is her congregation.'

'Oh, how lovely,' she said. 'Well, I won't keep you.' She turned to walk on.

'Actually, Miss Blackwell I was hoping I could speak with you,' Matthews said, getting straight to the point. 'It's regarding the article you're writing about Victor Crown.'

Clara paused before turning back to the detective. 'What about it?'

'As you know, I'm working on a case that involves him, and I'm curious if you've uncovered anything that might be relevant about him.'

Clara hesitated for a moment before speaking. 'Interesting.' She smirked.

'What is?'

'Wasn't it only yesterday morning you were telling me how my journalism was damaging and hurtful, and now suddenly you want my help.'

'Miss Blackwell, be reasonable.' Matthews sighed. 'This is a murder investigation and any information you have that can help solve the case could be valuable.'

'Well, I can tell you that Victor is not exactly the nicest person to work with,' she said. 'From what I've heard, he can be quite demanding and difficult to please.'

'That's not a surprise,' Matthews said, smiling. 'But is there anything more specific?'

'Well, I'm not sure how much I can tell you right now,' Clara said, a hint of reluctance in her voice. 'I don't want to compromise my sources.'

'I understand,' Matthews said. 'But if you do uncover anything that could help me with my case, I would appreciate it if you could let me know.'

'Of course,' Clara said with a smirk that irritated Matthews. 'I'll keep that in mind.'

Matthews watched as she entered the church. He didn't trust her; she had written many negative stories about him in the last few weeks, but he also knew any dirt she had on Victor could be useful.

Matthews took his seat in the front pew next to his sister, who now had baby Hugo in her arms. He was still fast asleep, and as the organ began to play loudly, Matthews was astonished it didn't wake him with a fright.

The sermon was about forgiveness and redemption, but Matthews couldn't help but let his mind wander. He kept glancing over at Clara, wondering how he could convince her to divulge the details of her article. As the service dragged on, he also found his mind wandering about Grace, and wondering what she was doing. He was hoping that she and Harvey were on the way home.

As the service ended and the congregation began to file out, Matthews and Charlotte lingered for a moment, waiting for John to finish playing the final song. Matthews felt a tap on his shoulder and turned to see Clara standing there, smiling at him.

'Miss Blackwell.' Matthews gave her a quizzical smile. 'Is everything all right?'

Clara leaned in slightly, keeping her voice low. 'The Plough Inn, on Baxtergate.'

'What of it?'

'Meet me outside tonight at nine o'clock.' Before Matthews could ask any more questions, she turned and walked back up the aisle and out of the church.

'What was all that about?' Charlotte asked.

'I have absolutely no idea.' Matthews frowned.

CHAPTER 8

Grace and Harvey had enjoyed a most comfortable night's sleep at Norton Conyers manor in their own private rooms with interconnecting doors. They enjoyed the luxury of a large four-poster bed and windows that looked over the grounds.

Lady Graham had insisted on feeding them a good breakfast before they made to leave. That morning, she no longer looked as though she was heading out to the stables but was dressed more elegantly. She donned an ensemble that defied convention, combining vibrant colours, elaborate accessories, and unexpected patterns in a harmonious yet delightfully unconventional fashion. Grace felt it was a lot of colours to take in so early on a Sunday morning.

'It is rare that I get to entertain,' she had told them across the large wooden dining table that had sixteen chairs around it and three candelabras on top which were currently unlit. Harvey was astonished by how polished the table was and couldn't stop looking at his reflection in the surface.

The breakfast spread consisted of fresh fruits, eggs, bacon, sausages, and a selection of pastries and cakes. Harvey had never seen so much food in one place. Lady Graham even insisted on them both wrapping some of the food up and taking it with them for the long journey back to Whitby.

Before they left, Harvey decided to leave a letter for George. Harvey had become a good reader, especially considering he had had no formal schooling. However, his writing was still in need of improvement, so he'd asked Grace to assist.

Sitting at a small writing desk in the manor's guest bedroom, Grace, with a pen and a sheet of paper in front of her, turned to Harvey, waiting for him to tell her what to write. There was a pause as Harvey mulled over what he wanted to say.

'Okay, Harvey. Let's get started,' she said. 'What do you want to say to your brother?' Harvey looked at the blank paper nervously.

'I want to tell him I'm sorry we didn't find him sooner and that I'm happy we finally met,' he said. 'I want him to know that I understand his reasons for not wanting to return to Whitby and if he doesn't want to be my brother, but I'll always be here for him if he changes his mind.'

Grace smiled softly. 'That's good. Now, let's see if I can put that into words on the paper.' She began to write, pausing occasionally to ask Harvey if he wanted to add anything.

'I know we didn't have the chance to grow up together, but I hope we can still get to know each other. I would like to write to you occasionally if I may?'

Grace smiled softly, her heart aching for the young boy who had longed for a connection with his brother. 'That's lovely, Harvey. Is there anything else?'

Harvey thought for a moment, his brow furrowed in concentration. 'Just that I hope we can meet again someday and get to know each other properly. That's all.'

Grace nodded and finished up the letter. She put down the pen and folded the paper neatly, placing it in an envelope with George's name written on the front. 'There we go. All done. Now we just have to leave it for George.'

Harvey's eyes shone with gratitude as he hugged Grace tightly, his small frame trembling with emotion. 'Thank you so much, Grace. I would have never found him without you.'

Grace hugged him back tightly. 'Of course, Harvey. You're family now, and family takes care of each other.'

They both sat in silence for a moment, holding onto each other. The letter was a small gesture, but it meant everything to Harvey.

Grace and Harvey made their way downstairs; it was time for them to leave. As they passed the sitting room, they saw Lady Graham sitting by the fireplace, reading a book.

Harvey was nervous as he approached her. She was a refined and elegant woman, with a sharp intelligence that Harvey found somewhat intimidating. She had been so kind and generous to them thus far; he didn't want to seem rude by asking her something else.

'Excuse me, Lady Graham.' He spoke softly as she looked up from her book. 'I have a letter I wish to leave behind for my brother, George,' he said, his voice shaking slightly. 'I was wondering if you could pass it on to him for me.'

'Of course, Harvey," she said, placing a comforting hand on his shoulder. 'I would be happy to help.' She placed her book on the side but kept hold of the envelope tightly as she walked them to the door and wished them well on their journey back to Whitby. 'I confess I am sad to see you both leave. It was lovely having the company last night.'

Their horse and carriage had been brought around to the front door, and Harvey opened the door for Grace to get inside first.

'Thank you for your hospitality, Lady Graham.' Grace smiled warmly from the carriage window. 'It's the first time either of us have stayed in such a grand house.'

'Thank you, Lady Graham,' Harvey added, beaming.

'You're welcome, my dears. And don't worry, I'll make sure George gets your letter, even if I have to read it to him myself,' she assured him.

'Oh… yes. Thank you,' Harvey replied. He had been so worried about what should be in the letter that he hadn't thought about whether George would be able to read it. He was now even more grateful that Lady Graham was such a kind-hearted woman. He felt hopeful that his brother might one day come around and accept him with Lady Graham's help.

The carriage began to move, and the sound of the horse hooves rang through the carriage. Grace and Harvey waved out of the window to Lady Graham, who was smiling with delight back at them.

Harvey and Grace settled into the carriage as it made its way down the winding driveway of Norton Conyers. Harvey was quiet, lost in thought as he watched the scenery pass by. Grace could tell he was thinking about George. She reached over and placed a comforting hand on his shoulder.

'Are you all right, Harvey?' she asked softly.

Harvey turned to her and gave a small smile. 'Yeah. I'm just glad we found him.'

'You know,' Grace began gently, 'it's a remarkable

thing that you found your brother at all. You should be really proud of yourself for all the work you put into finding him.'

Harvey's lips twitched into a bittersweet smile. 'Yeah, I suppose you're right. I can't quite believe we did it.'

Grace nodded. 'If you remember, you were shocked when you learnt of George. I'm sure he will be thinking of you, and the letter will help. George just needs some space to come to terms with everything.'

'I guess we'll see,' Harvey replied, feeling a mixture of relief and exhaustion at knowing his quest had come to an end.

As the carriage reached the gates of the estate, Harvey saw a gardener raking leaves; it was George. He watched his brother from a distance and sighed. No longer did he feel disappointment but was grateful that his hunt for George had finally been successful.

George heard the carriage and looked up from his work. The two brothers' eyes met, and Harvey unintentionally gave his brother a small wave goodbye. George's face softened, and a subtle smile of acknowledgement adorned his face as the carriage drove through the gates and out of sight.

CHAPTER 9

SUNDAY 27TH NOVEMBER 1892

The scent of a hearty Sunday roast filled the air as Detective Matthews sat around the dining table at his sister's house. The atmosphere was warm and familial, the clinking of cutlery and soft laughter mingling seamlessly.

Hugo, in his crib nearby, occasionally emitted a contented gurgle that drew a smile from Matthews, who gladly volunteered himself to sit beside his nephew. He found himself momentarily lost in the innocence of the baby's eyes, wondering if Grace and he would one day be blessed with their own son.

Charlotte's husband, John, leaned back in his

chair, his jovial voice filling the room with tales of work, but Matthews found himself zoning out of the conversation. Matthews nodded and feigned interest, occasionally stealing glances at his father, who was trying to change the subject and begin a spirited debate about politics with John.

The detective speared a piece of roasted potato on his plate, his mind wandering despite the lively chatter around him. As the conversation flowed, Matthews couldn't shake the itch of boredom that clung to him. He longed for Grace to return to Whitby. These meals always seemed more interesting when she was with him rather than the mundane small talk that seemed to dominate this meal.

'So, Benji,' Charlotte said with a fond smile, 'what did you think of John's playing in church today?'

Matthews tore his gaze away from Hugo and cleared his throat. 'It was... erm, good, Charlotte. Hymns, and erm... all that.'

John chimed in with a chuckle. 'You know, you could use a little more enthusiasm, Benjamin. Church isn't supposed to be a chore.'

Matthews offered a polite smile. 'Of course. It's

just that I find my thoughts are more often elsewhere.'

His father chuckled softly from his end of the table. 'Wandering thoughts, eh? Well, I suppose that's the plight of an active mind.'

Matthews nodded, glad for the change in topic. 'Indeed, Father.'

As the conversation continued, Matthews found himself growing restless. The conversation drifted to matters that held little interest for him—a new painting at the local gallery, the latest gossip from the neighbours. He stole glances at his pocket watch, subtly checking the time.

Hugo's laughter drew his attention back to the table, momentarily lifting his spirits. He enjoyed spending time with his nephew and was looking forward to when young Hugo was old enough to talk, walk, and much more.

After dessert was served, Matthews discreetly checked his watch once more. A feigned yawn escaped him. 'I apologize, everyone. It's been a long day, and I was up rather late working on a case.'

Charlotte looked apologetic. 'Oh, Benjamin. I'm sorry if we've kept you. Please don't feel obliged to stay if you're tired.'

Matthews, with a tinge of guilt, decided to take his sister up on the offer and made his excuses to leave.

He bid his farewells and made his way to the door, his sister walking him out. She watched him as he buttoned up his coat, and then she kissed him on the cheek in the doorway.

'Get home safe,' she said, watching him walk down the stone steps outside her home. He gave her a little wave before she closed the door.

Unwilling to return to an empty house just yet, Matthews decided to spend the remainder of the evening making enquiries about Alice Grey, Victor Crown's assistant.

His first port of call was to The White Horse and Griffin, one of the oldest inns in Whitby, situated on Church Street on the east coast of town. The small narrow bar area, with its exposed brick walls, wooden beams, and an open fireplace made it a cosy environment for any passing visitor to enjoy. The rooms, which were on the upper floors, were all of different shapes and sizes, with sloping wooden floors that creaked.

'May I help you?' came a voice from behind the bar as Matthews entered the inn.

'Ah, yes.' Matthews held out his hand. 'My name is Detective Matthews. I was wondering if you would be able to assist me with my investigation.'

'Of course.' The gentleman returned the handshake. 'I'm Mr Walker, the proprietor of the White Horse and Griffin.' He was a tall, thin man, with a lean face and a perfectly trimmed moustache. His dark hair too was perfectly managed to the point it looked as though it wouldn't move. His smart attire consisted of a white shirt, waistcoat, and jacket with a handkerchief poking out of the top pocket.

Matthews told Mr Walker about his investigation, and that he was looking to speak with Alice Grey. Mr Walker checked his diary obligingly, scanning the bookings he had.

'Here it is.' He stopped his finger halfway down the page. 'Yes, she has room nine. She arrived with two gentlemen. A Mr Victor Crown and a Mr Harry Denton, the latter of which booked the three rooms all on the same floor.'

'Have you seen Miss Grey today at all, Mr

Walker?'

'I can't say I have.' He spoke extremely softly. 'To tell the truth, I haven't seen her in a day or two, but that's quite common. I often miss my guests coming and going while I'm busy.'

'Would you be able to show me up to room nine?'

Mr Walker fetched a set of keys from behind the small bar and signalled for Matthews to follow him up the narrow staircase. They walked in silence, Mr Walker clearly not interested in making small talk. Upon arriving at room nine, Mr Walker gave a knock on the crooked wooden door. There was no answer, so he tried again, but there was still no answer. Mr Walker began unlocking the door, and as he opened it, he called out in case anybody was inside.

'Hello? It's just Mr Walker. Is anybody in here?' However, upon opening the door fully, it was clear the room was unoccupied.

Detective Matthews entered the empty room, his eyes scanning the space for any clues. The room was small and modest, with a bed, a chest of drawers, and a small table with a mirror above it. The curtains were drawn, and the room was dimly lit by the daylight filtering through the thin fabric. He noticed that the bed was unmade, and the window was slightly ajar, letting in a cool breeze that caused the curtains to sway gently.

The owner of The White Horse and Griffin stood awkwardly in the doorway, waiting for Matthews to finish his inspection. 'Is everything all right, Detective?' he asked, his voice laced with concern.

'Are you sure this is the right room?' Matthews asked, unable to see any personal possessions in the room that would suggest somebody was staying there.

'Absolutely, sir,' Mr Walker replied, fumbling with the cluster of keys in his hands. 'That's the name on the register. Alice Grey. She's been staying here since Wednesday. I showed her to the room myself.'

'And she hasn't checked out?'

'Not to my knowledge.'

Matthews asked Mr Walker to take him to the rooms of Victor Crown and Harry Denton. They were both sleeping in rooms on the same floor, and upon knocking on the neighbouring doors, they again were left unanswered. Matthews persuaded Mr

Walker to unlock the rooms for him, and this time, they were filled with multiple trunks and suitcases. Matthews gave the rooms a quick check-over while he had the opportunity, but again, didn't find anything out of the ordinary.

'Do you have housemaids that make over the rooms?' Matthews queried, noting that all three rooms had unmade beds.

'We had been given strict instructions not to interfere with the rooms and that they would inform me should they require anything.'

'Thank you for your help,' Matthews said, turning to the innkeeper. 'If you hear anything or if she comes back, please let me know.'

'Of course, sir,' Mr Walker replied, following Matthews out of Victor Crown's room and locking the door behind them.

As he walked down the stairs and out of the establishment, Matthews knew that speaking with Alice Grey could hold the answers he needed to solve this case. Had Alice fled town because she was involved in Bess Young's murder? Or was she simply afraid of getting caught up in the investigation? Either way, her sudden disappearance only fuelled his suspicions.

CHAPTER 10

SUNDAY 27TH NOVEMBER 1892

Detective Matthews adjusted his coat and hat, his reflection catching his gaze in the old brass-framed mirror in the hallway as he prepared to leave the house again. It was getting late, and even though darkness had descended, the rain's cacophonous symphony persisted against the window.

He was due to meet Clara Blackwell at the Plough Inn—a rendezvous he hoped was to discuss the ongoing investigation and whatever information she had on Victor Crown.

Just as he was about to grab the door handle to his front door, a firm knock echoed through the house, making him jump. Matthews furrowed his brows in surprise, pausing before he opened the door. Who could it be at this hour? He swung it open to find his friend, Jack, standing on the threshold, a sheepish grin on his face.

'Jack?' Matthews asked as his friend rushed through the door to get out of the rain. 'What brings you here?' He stepped aside to invite his friend in.

'Thought I'd drop by and keep you company,' Jack replied, water dripping off his coat and beard as he removed his hat. 'Figured you'd be all alone again this evening.'

Matthews chuckled, a hint of gratitude in his eyes. 'You're not wrong. However, I was just headed out to meet Clara Blackwell. I have some matters to discuss with her regarding the case.'

'Clara Blackwell?' Jack furrowed his brow, a perplexed expression crossing his features. 'I thought she was public enemy number one.' He chuckled. 'Since when do you get help from reporters?'

'She's been digging up dirt on Victor Crown for a tell-all article, and I want to know what she has on him.'

'Fair enough.' Jack sighed. 'I won't keep you, then.'

'You're more than welcome to come with me and join me for a drink,' said Matthews. 'I'm meeting her at the Plough Inn.'

'No, thanks.' Jack pulled a face. 'Not my kind of crowd.'

'Well, not since you became a married man,' Matthews teased.

Jack nodded, his eyes lingering on Matthews for a moment before he cleared his throat. 'Actually, there's something I've been wanting to tell you.'

Matthews raised an eyebrow, curious. 'Go on.'

'It's... well, about Beth.'

'What's the matter? Is she okay?' Matthews' expression turned to concern over Jack's wife.

Jack shifted on his feet, a mix of excitement and nervousness in his expression. 'Beth and I are expecting our first child.'

A smile broke across Matthews' face, genuine happiness radiating from his eyes. 'Jack, that's wonderful news! Congratulations!'

Jack's grin widened, relief flooding his features. 'Thank you. We've been keeping it a secret for a while now, and I was a little nervous to tell you.'

'Why?' Matthews blinked in surprise, momentarily taken aback by his friend's comment.

'Well, you know… you and Grace haven't had the best of times lately with, you know…' He didn't want to say the word *miscarriage* in case it upset his friend.

Matthews clapped a hand on Jack's shoulder. 'I'm truly happy for you both, as will Grace be. You should never worry about telling us such good news. This is a new chapter, and I have no doubt you'll make wonderful parents.'

Jack's gratitude was evident in his eyes as he nodded. 'Means a lot to hear that from you. Anyway, shall I walk you out?'

Matthews followed his friend out of the house and into the cold, wet night. They talked exclusively about the baby and how excited they were to meet the new addition when he or she finally arrived in the summer. Jack gave his farewells at the end of Baxtergate, leaving Matthews to head on up to the Plough Inn alone.

Baxtergate was mostly quiet now. Matthews guessed it was due to the weather. As he approached the Plough Inn, he saw Miss Blackwell huddled in a doorway, shielded from the rain, her face hidden under a hooded cloak.

'Detective, thank you for coming out in this weather,' she said, her voice raised over the howling wind.

'No problem,' he replied. 'But may I ask why you have dragged me out at this hour in the pouring rain instead of just meeting me in my dry office?'

'I have some information that may be useful in your investigation, but I wanted you to see something too.' She smirked.

'Miss Blackwell, why are you suddenly so keen on helping me?' Matthews' voice was stern. 'You have spent the last couple of months writing articles on how incompetent you think I am, and how I am in my position due to my father. So, forgive me if I'm a little wary of this sudden act of kindness.'

'I've told you before, Detective. I am a reporter and look only for the truth.' Her smirk had turned into a more serious expression. 'If anything I discover can help, then I will tell you, but if you would rather I leave.' She took a step out from under the covered doorway, but before she could take another, Matthews grabbed her by the arm and pulled her back.

'What have you got for me?' He didn't trust her, but he knew that if she had something useful, then he would be a fool to ignore it. 'Sorry.' He let go of her arm, realising he was still holding onto it.

Clara sighed. She gestured towards the pub window, where, inside, the bar area was filled with people. 'Can you see him?' She pointed through the glass.

'Who?'

'Timothy Young,' she replied with a sharp tone. Matthews leaned closer to the window, and towards the back of the bar was Timothy Young, flirting with a young waitress. 'I've been doing some digging, and it turns out Mr Young has been visiting this pub regularly. It's rumoured he's been having an affair with one of the barmaids. That one he currently has his arms around.'

Matthews frowned. 'Are you sure about that?' He continued to peer through the window. The pub was bustling, full of locals seeking refuge from the storm outside. The noise was carried out through the cracks in the old windows.

'Yes.'

'It might explain why he didn't seem that upset about the death of his wife, especially if he'd already emotionally moved on.' Matthews continued to stare through the window, watching Mr Young. In the corner of his eye, he spotted Harry Denton sitting at a small table in the far corner with a gentleman Matthews knew to be a drug dealer. Matthews found it odd how they seemed to be laughing and joking like old friends, despite Denton not being from Whitby.

'How did you come across this affair?' Matthews finally returned to face Clara.

'I followed him here last night, and after seeing his public displays towards the barmaid, I decided to ask the landlady if Mr Young was a regular visitor.'

'And what did she tell you?'

'She told me that Mr Young had always been a regular at the pub, and that it wasn't uncommon for him to flirt with the barmaids, despite being a married man.'

'Married men flirting with barmaids is hardly news,' Matthews replied.

'Maybe so, but she also told me that he had been

seeing one of her barmaids, a Miss Kathleen Metcalf, in secret for some time now. Potentially over a year.'

'You dragged me out into the rain to tell me that Timothy Young has been having an affair with a barmaid?' Matthews sighed. 'I thought you were going to tell me what dirt you have on Victor Crown.'

'I have yet to tell you the most interesting part, Detective,' Clara replied in a sarcastic tone.

'Oh?' Matthews looked at her with anticipation.

'Miss Kathleen Metcalf just so happens to be the younger sister of Bess Young.'

CHAPTER 11

Detective Matthews woke with a splitting headache. He had again been sitting up until the early hours of the morning, drinking and poring over his notes on the case. The last few days he had had nothing but the case to think about, and he was starting to realise how much he relied on Harvey for assistance.

As he dressed for work in his bedroom, he could hear the sound of a horse and carriage pulling up outside. He leaned over his wife's dressing table to see who it could be and was thrilled at the sight of Grace and Harvey emerging from the cab.

Matthews, in bare feet, trousers, and a shirt only

half buttoned up, rushed down the stairs just in time to see the pair of them walk through the front door. Matthews greeted his wife with a warm embrace. Grace gasped with surprise as Matthews lifted her into his arms before kissing her on the lips. He was grateful for her safe return, and he guessed from the smile on her face that the trip went well.

'Good morning, my love,' he said, returning her to the ground. 'I wasn't expecting you home until this evening at the earliest.'

'We decided to travel through the night.' She beamed through tired eyes. 'We were both eager to get home.'

'Was your trip a success?' Matthews hesitantly asked Harvey, leading them both into the sitting room.

Harvey began to speak in detail about their trip, and Matthews listened intently. He told Matthews all about the emotional reunion with George, the hospitality of Lady Graham, and how they had left a letter for him at Norton Conyers Manor. Yet, it was the manor house and sleeping in a four-poster bed that got Harvey the most animated, much to Matthews' amusement.

'That's great news,' Matthews said with a smile. 'I truly am happy that you found him, and I have every faith that he will write you back once he has had some time to process the news. It will have come as a shock to him to discover a brother he knew nothing about.'

Harvey looked pensive as Matthews spoke, his mind still lingering on the idea of reuniting with a lost family member. Grace noticed his expression and reached over to take his hand, offering a reassuring squeeze. 'You're right.' Harvey sighed. 'But if I don't hear from him, at least I know I tried.' Matthews placed a reassuring hand on Harvey's shoulder and said, 'Sometimes, Harvey, patience and time have a way of mending what's broken. Keep the door open, and you might be surprised one day to see him reaching out to you.' He gave Harvey a reassuring smile, and the hint of a smile on Harvey's face was all Matthews needed to see to know his young assistant was going to be okay.

Matthews cleared his throat. 'I'm heading to the station soon to continue with a new investigation. Harvey, you should rest after your long journey, but I will catch you up on it later today.'

'You can catch me up on the way to the station.' Harvey grinned. He was now living in the small lodgings above the police stable blocks. A single room, but one he had been able to call his own.

'I too should get ready for work.' Grace stood.

'Work?' Matthews' brows knitted together, his expression filled with genuine concern. 'Surely, you need to rest? I can go there on my way to the station and tell them you won't be in today.'

'Nonsense,' she hushed him. 'I'm only in half days on a Monday anyway. All will be fine.' Grace worked at a small dressmaker's a few days per week. She had always enjoyed the social side of it, and despite feeling tired, she was looking forward to getting back.

Matthews knew he would never win this argument but agreed to it only on the promise that he give her a ride on his way to the station in the carriage still waiting outside. They were waiting for Harvey to take them back to the station paddocks.

'Oh, before we leave.' Matthews' face turned serious. 'I have some news to share with you.'

Curiosity danced in Grace's gaze as she looked him in the eye. 'What is it?'

Matthews took a deep breath, his fingers drumming lightly on his knee. 'Jack came by last night. He wanted to tell me something important.'

Grace's brows furrowed with intrigue. 'And what did he say?'

A mixture of emotions swirled within him. He knew Grace's recent miscarriage had been a painful blow for both of them, and he approached the topic with caution. 'He and Beth are expecting a baby, due in the early summer.'

For a moment, Grace's expression faltered, a shadow of sadness passing over her features. Matthews held his breath, bracing himself for her reaction.

To his surprise, a genuine smile emerged on Grace's lips. 'That's wonderful news, Benjamin. I'm truly happy for them. Beth should be at work today too. I'll make sure to congratulate her.'

With that, Grace stood and headed back out of the sitting room to where her luggage had been left by the front door. With the aim of taking it upstairs, Matthews quickly appeared in the hallway and took it from her, then helped her upstairs with her things.

A short time later, Matthews, Grace, and Harvey

got into the carriage to take Grace to work. During the short ride, Matthews told them briefly about his new case. 'I was thinking about getting us tickets to see the Victor Crown show tomorrow night,' he said, and Harvey's eyes lit up with excitement.

Grace paused and bit her lip as she looked at her husband with concern in her eyes. 'Is it safe?'

'Of course. The man is simply an illusionist,' Matthews reassured her. 'It wasn't the show that killed Bess Young, it was somebody later that night. Anyway, I thought you'd be happy. You spoke a lot about Victor Crown when the show was first announced.'

'Still, I'm not so sure us being there when the performer and his assistant are under investigation is a good idea.'

'Trust me.' Matthews placed his hand in hers. 'Everything is going to be all right, and we'll enjoy an entertaining performance.'

'I'm not sure.' Grace gave a hesitant smile.

Matthews decided not to push it any further. Grace had barely been leaving the house other than for her job the last few months. Ever since the miscarriage, she had become a shell of her former self, choosing to stay home over joining in with social events. What began as her unwillingness to hear more expressions of sympathy evolved into her gradual withdrawal from social interactions. So, Matthews wasn't surprised by her reluctance to attend the theatre; he understood the need to approach the idea of her doing more outside of the house delicately and persist gently without rushing her.

They dropped Grace off at the little dress shop and headed towards the station.

'What is it you're not telling me?' Harvey asked once Grace had left.

'What do you mean?'

'I got the impression you didn't tell us everything you know.'

'You're both tired. I hardly wish to overload you with all the facts right now,' Matthews assured.

'Well, I slept in the carriage on the way home, so I feel fine. You can tell me everything so I can get back to helping you.' Harvey had never spoken so sternly to Matthews before, and for a split second, he was worried he had overstepped the mark. Matthews, however, was continuously impressed with his enthusiasm to learn and grow and spent the short journey telling him everything he had uncovered so far, including the help he had been getting from Clara Blackwell.

'Clara Blackwell!' Harvey spat. 'Why would you ask her for help?'

'As always, she has been poking around, looking for a story,' Matthews began. 'I discovered Miss Blackwell is writing a tell-all piece about Victor Crown, and I asked her what dirt she had on him, that's all.'

'And what did she have?'

'She refuses to disclose that information.' Matthews pursed his lips. 'She is an investigator in her own way, following people and getting information on them from so-called sources. She could prove to be useful if we keep her on a tight leash.'

Harvey let out an audible gasp. 'You wish to work with her more?' His voice reached an unusually high tone in his apparent shock.

'Ideally not, but if she can get information without being noticed, then she could have her uses. We just need to convince her to share what she has.'

'So, what's the plan?' Harvey asked as he and

Matthews began unhooking the horses from the carriage in the middle of the station courtyard.

'We need to find Alice Grey. I get the feeling she hasn't gone very far. Victor will have told her to lie low until this all blows over. We also need to speak with Bess's younger sister about this alleged affair.' Matthews paused.

'Do you think the affair could have something to do with Bess's murder?'

'It wouldn't be the first time death has occurred over a love triangle.'

They finished putting away the horses and made their way up the Matthews' office. 'What would you like me to start on?' asked Harvey.

Matthews thought for a moment. 'Actually, there is something you can do. If you're sure you don't need to rest up first.'

'I'm okay. I want to do something.'

'Okay, Alice Grey seems to have gone into hiding. I searched her room at The White Horse and Griffin yesterday, and it had been cleared out. We need to find and talk to her. Maybe you could ask around and see if anyone knows where she is.'

'Surely, she would have left town.'

'We can't be certain.' Matthews frowned as he juggled with his thoughts. 'The landlord had no idea she had left, and most guests would require a carriage to help them with their baggage. Also, I get the impression that Victor's manager keeps the money close to himself, so I would be surprised if she had much money on her, unless Victor gave her some.'

'I'll ask around.' Harvey headed for the door.

'Meet me at The Plough Inn this evening,' Matthews called after him. 'I want us to speak with Bess's sister, and I thought you could join me.' Matthews had missed his work partner and was looking forward to having the company again.

'Okay!' Harvey called as he raced out of the door.

CHAPTER 12

Detective Matthews leaned against the wall outside The Plough Inn, checking his pocket watch every few seconds. The inn was still closed, and he had arrived early, hoping to catch Kathleen Metcalf before her shift began. He had a few questions for her about her sister and was hoping she could shed some light on the investigation.

It was already dark, and the only light came from the gas street lamps that lined the road. The cold late afternoon meant the street was much quieter than it would normally be. Most of the shops on Baxtergate would be closing soon, and the pub would be bursting with people in no time.

'Detective, I hope you're not planning on standing there all evening and scaring away my punters.' It was Mrs Penn, the landlady of The Plough Inn. She was a tall, thin woman with black curly hair and a face that was always fully made up. She had bangles up both arms that jingled and rattled so much that it was easy to hear her coming.

'You've no need to worry, Mrs Penn. I'm just waiting to speak to one of your waitresses about a case I'm working on.'

'Oh, yes?' She replied with a sudden interest, while unlocking the door and placing out a blackboard with a list of beers and ales for sale. 'Who's that, then?'

'Miss Kathleen Metcalf.'

'Oh, I see.' Mrs Penn stopped what she was doing and faced the detective, her face now pouting as though ready to gossip. 'I did hear about her sister, poor thing. Mind you, I heard her husband wasn't afraid to beat her, even in public, so God bless her for finally being at peace, I say.' Mrs Penn didn't wait for Matthews to respond and wandered back into the pub where he could see her through the window, lighting candles on the tables before lighting a small open fire in the corner.

'Beat her?' Matthews whispered to himself, wondering if this was idle gossip or if there was some truth in it.

As Matthews continued to wait, Harvey appeared, looking tired but determined.

'You should have stayed home and rested,' Matthews told him as he walked towards him.

'I'm all right,' Harvey replied, though a yawn as he said it did not help his case.

'Any luck finding Alice?' Matthews asked, hoping for some good news.

Harvey shook his head. 'No, I'm afraid not. Nobody seems to know where she is. I've checked around different boarding houses. I asked at the train station if any of the staff had seen her boarding a train, but she's nowhere to be found.'

'Victor will have told her to flee, then.' Matthews sighed, frustrated. Alice was a key witness in the case, and her unwillingness to testify could cost them the entire investigation. 'Thanks for trying, Harvey. I will send word to officers in York, Leeds, and beyond to keep a look out for her. She's bound to turn up somewhere.'

After a few minutes, a young woman approached the pub, and Matthews immediately recognised her as Kathleen Metcalf. She possessed a delicate beauty, her porcelain skin a contrast to her dark, cascading curls. Her eyes held a hint of mystery, framed by long lashes that fluttered with every glance. She wore a gown of muted blue, its intricate lacework tracing delicate patterns across the bodice and sleeves, perfectly complementing her demure presence.

'Good evening, Miss Metcalf,' Matthews said, approaching her with caution. She stopped in her tracks and looked at him as though disturbed from a deep thought. 'My name is Detective Matthews, and this is my colleague, Harvey. We were hoping to speak with you about your sister, Bess.'

Kathleen looked wary but nodded. 'Sure. What do you want to know?'

'Could we maybe go on inside? This shouldn't take long.'

Kathleen nodded and led them inside the cold, poorly lit pub. Mrs Penn was behind the bar and, upon seeing the detective with Kathleen, offered them into a small back room to speak privately, worried that Matthews interviewing people for a case in the middle of her bar would look bad for business.

Matthews sat across from Kathleen at a small table. He leaned forward, taking out his pen and notebook from his satchel, ready to take notes on any information that she would reveal about her sister's death. Harvey continued to stand. Too tired to get involved, he stood back and let Matthews interview her alone.

'I have been tasked with the job of finding out what happened to your sister, and I was wondering if you would be able to tell me anything about her that might help me with my investigation.'

Kathleen's face darkened at the mention of her sister. 'I don't know anything,' she said, her voice tinged with anger.

'Miss Metcalf,' Matthews continued, 'I understand that this is a difficult time for you. I appreciate your willingness to speak with me.'

Kathleen's lips tightened, and her gaze flickered towards Matthews before quickly darting away. 'I don't know what I can tell you. Bess... she was my sister, but we weren't close.'

Matthews noted the bitterness that laced her words. 'Could you tell me a little about your relationship with Bess?'

Kathleen's fingers clenched around a shabby handkerchief she had pulled from her handbag. 'We were never particularly close, even when we were younger. She always wanted more attention, more recognition. And now, with her gone, people are acting like she was some sort of saint.'

Matthews observed the mixture of frustration and sadness in Kathleen's eyes. 'I understand that emotions can run high during times like this. Were there any recent interactions or disagreements between you?'

Kathleen's gaze finally met his, and there was a hint of vulnerability in her expression. 'We had a fight. The night before she... died. Over something trivial, really. But it was the way she looked at me, like she was so disappointed. And then she stormed off.'

Matthews' tone was gentle. 'Would you mind sharing what the argument was about?'

Kathleen's grip on the handkerchief tightened

even further. 'It's embarrassing. She accused me of trying to take Timothy away from her. But that's ridiculous.'

Detective Matthews took a deep breath and leaned forward. 'Miss Metcalf, I have to ask you about your relationship with Timothy Young.'

Kathleen's face turned pale, and her eyes widened with surprise. 'My relationship with him?'

'Yes.' Matthews talked calmly. 'I have reason to believe that you and Mr Young were more than just...'

'I don't know what you're talking about,' she interrupted.

'Miss Metcalf, I have it on good authority that you and Mr Young have been engaged in a more intimate affair for some time now. Would this be correct?'

Kathleen took a deep breath and then began to cry. 'I'm sorry.' Her face was streaked with tears, and her eyes quickly became red and puffy as she cried uncontrollably.

'You don't need to apologise to me.' Matthews pulled out a clean handkerchief from his coat pocket and handed it to her. 'I just need you to tell me the truth. Now, did Bess know about this affair?'

Kathleen wiped her tears, her shoulders slumped in defeat. 'Yes, she found out,' she whispered. 'Tim and I were always very careful, and we never did anything that would give us away. I know Tim had been unhappy for a long time. We never meant for it to happen. But Bess was devastated when she found out. She never forgave me.'

'And how did Timothy react when Bess found out?' Matthews asked.

'He was angry,' Kathleen said. 'He accused Bess of spying on him and said she was being paranoid. But I could tell he was worried. He knew Bess was capable of doing something drastic.'

'Drastic?' Matthews queried. 'How drastic?'

'Oh, I simply mean break his possessions or something like that.' Kathleen sniffled. 'She was always over dramatic, even at the slightest thing.' Matthews couldn't help but be intrigued by how casually Kathleen discussed the affair, as if being involved with your sister's husband was a trivial matter.

'They attended the theatre together. Does that mean she forgave him?'

'Publicly, yes, but I don't think she had gotten over it really.'

'So, is this what the fight between you two was about? Because she found out?'

'Oh, no.' Kathleen sniffed. 'She found out months ago. We hadn't spoken since, until the night before her death.'

'May I ask if you continued to see Mr Young after your sister learnt of the affair?'

'Not straight away,' Kathleen pursed her lips. 'I didn't see him for over two weeks, and then one night, he showed up drunk. We didn't sleep together that night, but we did start to see each other again more over the following weeks.'

'So, this new argument was about something else?' Matthews asked with a frown.

'Not exactly.' Kathleen looked somewhat sheepish as she spoke, her gaze often shifting away from Detective Matthews, 'Tim had returned home drunk and told her...' She hesitated. 'It's embarrassing.'

'Go on.'

'He told her he wished he hadn't married the barren sister.' Kathleen dropped her gaze.

'Had Mr Young mentioned leaving his wife for you? Had you asked him to?'

'He told me he didn't believe in divorce, and that he took a vow until death.' She sniffled before looking up at Matthews in concern over what she had just said.

'Have you seen Mr Young since your sister's death?' Matthews quickly continued.

'Err, well, yes, of course.' Kathleen hesitated. 'I've checked on him a couple of times, and he came to the bar too.'

Matthews scribbled down some notes. 'Miss Metcalf, can you think of any reasons somebody would wish to harm your sister?'

Kathleen nervously fidgeted with her hands, her eyes flickering around the room. 'Bess had debts,' she admitted, her voice barely above a whisper. 'She was getting threatening letters about them.'

'Threatening letters.' Matthews raised an eyebrow. 'Can you tell me more about these debts and who might have sent the letters?'

'I don't know much,' Kathleen replied, shaking her head. 'Bess was always secretive about her finances, and as I mentioned, we barely spoke, so I only ever heard about it from Tim.'

'Did Mr Young mention who she owed the money to?' Matthews asked.

Kathleen shook her head.

Matthews made a note of this in his notebook before asking his next question. 'What was Bess's relationship with her husband like?'

Kathleen's face twisted in a pained expression. 'It was complicated. They had been trying for children for years, but it wasn't happening. It put a strain on their marriage, especially when Tim started drinking heavily. They argued a lot.'

'Did Bess ever confide in you about Tim's drinking or their problems with starting a family?' Matthews asked.

Kathleen nodded slowly. 'Yes. I'm her sister. She used to tell me a lot before she found out about the affair. But she didn't want me to interfere. She thought they could work it out on their own. As they drifted apart, Tim started hanging out at the bar more and more, and we found ourselves talking often.'

'Do you know of any times Mr Young hit his wife?' Matthews asked, remembering the comment from the landlady.

'Not that I know of.' Kathleen looked Matthews back in the eye. 'We might not have been on good terms, but I would have stuck up for her if I'd known about that.'

Matthews stood from the table. 'Thank you, Miss Metcalf. You've been very helpful. If you think of anything else, please don't hesitate to contact me.'

As Kathleen left, Matthews slumped back in his chair, looked at Harvey, and let out a sigh.

'She knows more than she's telling us,' Harvey said.

'I couldn't agree more.' Matthews reached into his satchel and pulled out his notepad and pencil.

'Did you see her eyes flicker after she mentioned "until death do us part", or however she worded it.' Harvey rested his hands on top of the now vacant chair opposite Matthews. 'She realised exactly what she'd said about a dead woman, and how that sounds to a detective investigating a murder.'

'I did notice.' Matthews smirked. 'And you, Harvey, are certainly getting the hang of this game.'

CHAPTER 13

MONDAY 28TH NOVEMBER 1892

Matthews walked through the front door of his home, the sound of his shoes tapping against the wooden floor echoing through the hallway. The house was cold, and there were no lights coming from any of the downstairs rooms. The flickering light of a candle could be seen at the top of the stairs, indicating to Matthews that Grace was already in the bedroom. He hung his coat on the rack and climbed the squeaky wooden staircase. He was tired after yet another long day, but he was glad to be home.

He found Grace dressed in her nightgown, sitting at her dresser and brushing her long blonde hair in front of the mirror. Matthews walked up to her and placed a soft kiss on her cheek, but she didn't respond with the usual warmth he was used to. She remained silent, continuing to brush her hair without looking at him. Their relationship had become more and more like this these past few months.

'Are you all right, love?' Matthews asked, concerned as he began to undress for bed.

Grace let out a deep sigh. 'I'm fine,' she said, her voice flat.

Matthews knew she wasn't fine. Ever since her miscarriage, she had been distant, barely speaking to him. He had been trying to give her space, but it seemed like it wasn't helping.

'Good news for Harvey,' he continued. 'You too must be pleased the search has finally come to an end.'

'Yes, I suppose so.'

'How was Beth? Did you tell her Jack had told us their news?'

'Uh-huh.'

'Grace… we need to talk,' Matthews said gently, sitting down on the edge of the bed directly beside her chair.

'Harvey told you everything about the meeting with his brother.' She continued brushing her hair. 'I don't think there's anything more to tell you.'

'Not about that.' Matthews reached out for her hand, but she quickly withdrew it. She placed the hairbrush back onto the dresser and made to leave. Matthews also stood and tried to block her path. 'Grace, we can't just ignore what happened,' he said firmly. 'I know it's difficult, but we need to face it together.'

'I don't want to talk about it,' Grace replied, still not looking at him. 'I can't face it. It's too painful.' A tear escaped Grace's eye, tracing a glistening path down her cheek. She wiped it away, her gaze returning to the floor.

Matthews felt a pang of sadness in his chest. He hated seeing her like this. Standing in front of her, he gently took both of her hands in his. 'I understand it's painful, Grace. But we're in this together. We can't let this come between us.'

Grace finally looked up at him, tears in her eyes. It was the first time she had looked him in the eye for what seemed like weeks. 'I know,' she said softly.

'I just don't know how.'

Matthews pulled his wife into an all-encompassing hug, her tears now falling against his bare chest. They stood there embracing for what seemed like hours, both falling silent in each other's arms, the tension in the room palpable.

'I just don't know what to say.' Grace sighed, breaking the silence. 'I feel like a failure. I can't give you a child.'

'Hey, don't say that,' Matthews said, rubbing her back as they continued to embrace. 'We'll get through this together. You're not a failure. You're my wife, and I love you.'

'I love you too. But it's just hard. I feel like I'm supposed to be over it by now, but I'm not.'

Matthews touched her chin and gently raised her face to look up at him. 'It's okay to not be okay, Grace. We'll take all the time we need.'

Matthews gestured for her to sit on the bed, and he sat beside her, one hand around her waist and the other holding her hand. He waited patiently, in case she wanted to say anything more. They sat in silence for a few moments before Matthews spoke up again. 'You know you can talk to me about anything. You don't need to keep it all inside.'

'I know,' Grace said softly. 'I'm sorry. I'm just having a hard time opening up about this.'

'I understand,' Matthews said, kissing her forehead. 'But please don't shut me out completely. I love you.'

Grace gave him a small smile, the first one he had seen in weeks. 'I love you too,' she said, leaning in for a kiss.

Matthews wrapped his arms around her, holding her tightly. He knew they had a long road ahead of them, but he was determined to get through it with Grace by his side.

'Let's do something this week. Get out of the house,' Grace said, drying her eyes.

'What were you thinking?' Matthews was surprised. They had done very little together socially for the past couple of months.

'I did think it might be nice to see the Victor Crown show if there are tickets still available.'

'Are you sure?'

'Yes.' Matthews was certain he could see a small twinkle in her eyes. 'I haven't been out of the house other than for work in such a long time. It'll be good to get dressed up for the theatre.'

'Okay, then.' Matthews kissed her on the cheek. 'I will see if I can get us tickets for tomorrow night.'

Matthews stood and pulled back the bed covers to make room for them to get into bed. He was slightly uncertain as Grace had been spending many nights in the spare bedroom. He could sense her hesitation as she stood by the bed.

'I don't know if I can. I don't know if I'm ready for… you know,' she whispered.

'I expect nothing from you other than seeing you sleep soundly.' He held out a hand to her.

'I just don't want to hurt us again,' Grace said softly.

'You could never hurt me. We will take it slowly, one night at a time. We don't have to do anything you don't want to.'

Grace looked at him and smiled slightly. 'Thank you.' She took his hand and joined him in bed. Matthews placed the covers over her and placed his arm around her.

They settled into bed together, holding each other close. Matthews could feel the weight of the topic still lingering between them, but he didn't want to push her to talk about it anymore. Instead, he focused on the feel of her body against his, the rise and fall of her chest, and the warmth of her skin. He had missed her touch.

As they lay there, Matthews couldn't help but worry about the state of their relationship. He loved Grace more than anything, but he knew they needed to work through this difficult time together. He hoped that, in time, they would be able to find their way back to each other fully, stronger and more connected than ever before.

For now, though, he was content just to hold her close and let her know he was there for her, no matter what.

CHAPTER 14

As Detective Matthews woke from a deep sleep, he noticed Grace was no longer in the bed next to him. A momentary panic saw him sit up quickly and scan the room, just as Grace re-entered the bedroom still wearing her nightgown.

'Sorry.' She smiled. 'Did I wake you?'

'No.' Matthews yawned. 'I didn't hear you leave.'

Grace placed a hot tea in a delicate china cup with a floral pattern on the side table next to her husband, kissing him as she passed. Matthews was surprised to see her looking so upbeat. Clearly, their discussion the night before had been a huge weight off her shoulders.

He knew he needed to get up and start the day, but as Grace returned to bed, he found himself drawn to her and the warmth of the bed. He placed his arm around her, and without realising it, fell back to sleep.

A loud knock on the front door downstairs startled them. 'What time is it?' Matthews reached passed his now cold cup of tea for his pocket watch. It had been nearly an hour since Grace had returned to the room with his morning drink. 'Shit.'

He jumped out of bed and hopped over to the window. He leaned over the dressing table to look out of the window and saw Harvey waiting at the kerbside with a horse and carriage.

'Always punctual, isn't he?' Grace knew who it was without Matthews saying a word.

'Eager.' Matthews chuckled. He quickly put on some trousers and threw a shirt on before darting out of the bedroom without doing up any of the buttons. He raced downstairs barefoot and threw open the front door. 'Come on inside, Harv,' Matthews called to him as he turned on his heels and retreated back up the stairs. 'I'm almost ready.

Would you like anything to eat or drink?'

'No, thank you, Detective,' Harvey shouted up the stairs to him, his voice echoing in the hallway.

Matthews finished getting dressed, put on his shoes, and kissed Grace, who sat up in bed watching him finish getting ready. 'I hope you have a good day,' she called after him.

When Matthews returned downstairs, he found Harvey still waiting for him in the hallway. He looked a lot fresher after a good night's sleep. The long journey from Norton Conyers with nothing, but an uncomfortable carriage to sleep in wouldn't have done either of them any favours.

Matthews grabbed his coat and followed Harvey out the door. Whitby stood shrouded in a relentless downpour, the bitter cold of the wind seeping through every crack and crevice of the town.

'Where to first?' Harvey asked.

'I want us to pay a visit to Timothy Young's house. We need to ask him some more questions, plus, I would like to look through Bess's belongings if he will allow me. After her sister's claims that she had been receiving threatening letters, I'd like to see if we can find them.'

The carriage ride to Timothy Young's house on the East Cliff side of town was not a long one, and with the weather as bad as it was, the streets were quieter than usual. Mr Young lived at the end of Green Lane, in a small stone-built cottage. There were similar-looking cottages on either side of his, and a small infant school directly across the road built using the same stone.

He rang the doorbell and waited, the silence only broken by the distant sound of workers in the Wharf just a few hundred metres away and seagull's calls being carried along in the howling of the wind. After a few moments, the door creaked open just wide enough for Matthews to see just the sliver of Mr Young's face. Upon realising who it was, Timothy opened the door wider, looking at Matthews and Harvey with a mixture of suspicion and apprehension. He looked dishevelled and hungover, and the stench of body odour and tobacco reeked from the doorway. Matthews re-introduced himself and asked for a follow-up interview about his wife's murder.

'Of course,' Timothy said, with hesitation. 'Please, come in.'

Matthews and Harvey followed him into the small living room. The house was cold, damp, and unkempt, and the small living room was a chaotic jumble of mismatched furniture and scattered belongings, as if a whirlwind of disarray had swept through. Cigarette buds and ash were littered everywhere. Timothy sat in an armchair and offered them a seat, but Matthews politely declined and remained standing. Harvey lingered in the doorway.

'Since our last conversation, Mr Young, I was wondering if you had any more thoughts regarding the investigation?'

Mr Young shook his head. 'No. I can't think of anyone who would want to hurt Bess. She was a kind woman, loved by everyone who knew her. Clearly a drunk or a pervert. She was probably just in the wrong place at the wrong time.'

'Mr Young, can you tell me about your relationship with Kathleen Metcalf?'

'Well... erm...' Timothy's eyes widened, and he appeared utterly taken aback by the unexpected question, his brows furrowing and his mouth slightly agape. 'She's Bess's sister. What does she have to do with all this?'

'I have reason to believe that the two of you have a romantic relationship,' Matthews said, his tone firm but not accusatory.

Timothy Young's face paled, and he looked like he was about to faint. 'I don't know what you're talking about,' he stammered. 'How dare you come into my home and accuse me of such things with zero evidence?'

'I'm afraid we have evidence to suggest otherwise,' Matthews said. 'In the form of a confession from Miss Metcalf herself. You see, I interviewed her yesterday regarding the case.'

Timothy's eyes widened. 'I... I don't know what to say,' he muttered, his voice barely audible.

'Mr Young, could your involvement with Miss Metcalf possibly have any relevance to your wife's tragic demise?'

Tim's eyes darted back and forth as he considered the question. 'No. No, of course not,' he said, shaking his head vigorously. 'I loved my wife. I would never do anything to hurt her.'

'Can I ask how long this affair had been going on before Bess's murder?'

Tim lowered his head, clearly embarrassed to be

answering these kinds of questions. 'Over a year. Maybe close to two.'

'Where did you meet up with Miss Metcalf?' Matthews asked. 'I'm guessing you didn't bring her back to the marital home.'

'No,' Tim mumbled. 'It started in the early summer last year.' He sighed and continued to look at the floor. 'We sometimes met in the gardens of Folly House, just at the top of Green Lane, and sometimes we met in the graveyard at the church closest to her house.' His voice was shaking. 'Then, when winter arrived and it got cold, I would visit her at The Plough Inn, where she works. They have rooms there, where gentlemen...'

'I am perfectly aware of what goes on behind those doors, thank you, Mr Young.' Matthews cut him off. He studied Tim's face carefully, looking for any signs of deception. He didn't see any, but he couldn't be sure. 'I'm sorry to have to ask these questions, but we have to consider all possibilities.' Timothy nodded but continued to look down at the floor. 'Mr Young, may I ask what you do for a living?'

'I'm employed by the Parish as a town husband.'

'What's that?' Harvey interrupted.

'A town husband is somebody who is employed by the parish to collect money from the fathers of illegitimate children, for their upkeep.'

'Have you held this position for long?' Matthews asked.

'It'll be coming up ten years, I would think.'

'Do you and Mrs Young have any children?'

'No.' Mr Young's eyes welled with sorrow, his shoulders slumped, and his face bore an unmistakable expression of profound sadness at this comment, and it was clear he had no intentions of delving any deeper into that conversation.

Matthews changed the topic. 'Mr Young, we also have reason to believe that Bess had some debts and was receiving threatening letters about them. Do you know anything about this?'

Timothy finally looked up and straight into Matthews' face. 'No, I had no idea. She never mentioned anything like that to me.' Matthews held his silence, and Timothy cast his eyes downward once again. Matthews couldn't help but recall Kathleen's claim that she had learned about the debts from Timothy. This left the detective pondering which of the two might be lying to him.

Matthews then asked if he could search Bess's belongings for any clues that might help with the investigation. Mr Young hesitated for a moment but eventually nodded his consent.

'Of course. Anything that can help,' he said.

'Harvey, this will work quicker if we split up,' Matthews said. Harvey, who had so far been standing by the living room door, quietly jumped at the mention of his name. 'You search the living room and kitchen, and I will look upstairs.'

Timothy's face twisted into an expression of sudden concern as he contemplated the idea of both Harvey and Matthews rifling through his belongings. As Matthews exited the room, making his way toward the staircase, the conflicted emotions on Timothy's face were evident. He seemed torn between following Matthews upstairs or remaining behind to keep a watchful eye on Harvey.

Matthews began his search of the bedroom, looking through Bess's wardrobe and drawers as well as under the bed. She didn't have many belongings. He checked the floorboards in case any came away to reveal a hidden compartment, but he found nothing of significance in the entire room.

'Detective,' Harvey called from downstairs. 'You may want to see this.' Matthews raced down the stairs to find Harvey covered in soot, a small metal tin clasped in his hands. 'I found it lodged behind the fireplace.' Harvey handed the tin over to Matthews and tried to brush himself down, but that only made the soot spread across him further.

Timothy, who had remained in the living room watching Harvey, looked on nervously, his expression telling Matthews that he didn't recognise the box. He walked over to Matthews so he too could see what was inside the tin with a limp in his step Matthews hadn't noticed up until then.

'Are you hurt?' Matthews asked.

'Oh, no,' Mr Young stuttered. 'Just gout that flares up from time to time.'

'That's usually a rich man's ailment, is it not?'

'True, though apparently, you can also get it from too much alcohol.' Mr Young avoided eye contact with the detective and instead looked at the tin grasped in Matthews' hands.

Matthews opened the tin and found a collection of letters addressed to Bess. The letters were written in a sinister tone and threatened Bess with harm if she didn't pay her debts.

'What do they say?' Timothy asked, trying to lean over the detective to get a better look. Matthews read aloud the top letter.

'Mrs Young, your deadline to make the payment has passed, and we are now left with no choice but to take action. It's vital that you pay off your debts immediately or face the consequences. We suggest that you do not make things worse for yourself by continuing to ignore your responsibilities. You have until Friday. C.H.G.' Matthews looked up from the letter. 'And it's dated four days before Bess's murder.'

'Who is C.H.G?' Harvey asked, looking at Matthews and Mr Young.

'I have no idea,' Timothy replied, looking at the detective with concern.

'Did you have any ideas at all that your wife was in debt, Mr Young?' Matthews folded the letters and returned them to the tin.

'No.' Mr Young's voice was shaky. 'Do you think that this C.H.G. person is responsible?'

'Mr Young, if I may, I will take these letters back with me to the station.' Matthews placed the tin into his oversized coat pocket and headed for the door. 'Should you recall anything further that may help with the investigation, I implore you to come and speak to me.'

Timothy nodded and followed Matthews and Harvey to the front door. He stood and watched on as they left his house and returned to their carriage parked outside.

'Do you know who C.H.G. is?' Harvey whispered to Matthews unsure if Mr Young was out of earshot.

'Charles Henry Gaskell. He's a well-known loan shark in town. The police have been trying to shut him down for years now.'

'How would Bess Young get involved with somebody like him?'

'I don't know, Harvey.' Matthews sighed. 'But people don't just borrow money from a loan shark unless they are desperate. We need to find out why she needed the money, and what happened to it.'

CHAPTER 15

etective Matthews and Harvey stood outside the imposing house of Charles Henry Gaskell, the man Matthews suspected to be the loan shark behind the threatening letters sent to Bess Young. Its grand façade rose tall and solemn, its windows reflecting the overcast sky like sombre mirrors.

They climbed the stone steps and approached the heavy oak door. Matthews raised his hand and knocked, the sound echoing through the quiet street. Moments later, the door creaked open, revealing a tall and imposing figure—a middle-aged man with receding hair, a sharp gaze, and a face marked by deep lines and shrewd eyes. It was Charles Henry Gaskell, the personification of a shady figure. He regarded the detective and Harvey with a mixture of curiosity and suspicion.

'Can I help you, gentlemen?' Gaskell inquired, his voice carrying an air of guarded caution.

Detective Matthews stepped forward, his gaze piercing into Gaskell's eyes. 'Good day, Mr Gaskell. I am Detective Benjamin Matthews, and this is my assistant, Harvey. We'd like to speak with you regarding a matter of great importance.'

Gaskell's eyes flickered with wariness. 'What is this about?'

'We believe you may have been involved in sending threatening letters to a woman named Bess Young,' Matthews stated firmly, his voice filled with authority.

Gaskell's face contorted with feigned innocence. 'I assure you, I have no idea what you're talking about. I have never sent threatening letters to anyone.' He folded his arms across his chest. 'I run a legitimate business here, Detective, I assure you.'

Matthews held his gaze, his intuition telling him otherwise. 'Mrs Young received explicit threats demanding payment for her debts. We have attained these letters which are signed with your initials, Mr Gaskell.' Matthews' gaze remained unyielding. 'On Friday night, Mrs Young was found dead. If you cooperate, we can resolve this matter peacefully. Refuse, and I'll have no option but to issue a warrant for your arrest.'

A flicker of unease crossed Gaskell's face before he composed himself, wearing a mask of confidence. 'Dead?' he spat. 'Look, Detective, I'm a businessman. I deal in legitimate loans. If someone fails to repay their debts, it's not my responsibility. I do not, however, resort to murder. How the fuck do you think I would get the money back from somebody if they are dead? Look,' he took a breath and regained his composure, 'I may have lent her some money, but it's all legal. She owed me a substantial amount, and I was merely trying to collect what was rightfully mine. Anyway, her debt was paid before Friday, so I had no reason to be looking for her.'

'It was paid?' Matthews interjected. 'By who?'

'By her.'

'But how?'

'Believe it or not, Detective, I am not one for making friends with my clients or partaking in casual small talk. So how she came by the money has nothing to do with me, nor is her murder. So, if that is all…'

Harvey, who had been observing silently, spoke up. 'But the threatening letters, Mr Gaskell. Are you saying you had no part in sending them either?'

Gaskell's eyes darted from Harvey to Matthews. He sighed, defeated. 'All right, I admit it. I sent those letters. I wanted to put some pressure on her to pay up. It was just a tactic that usually works with those trying to fob me off.'

Matthews pulled out a letter from his pocket. 'May I ask you what you meant by the term, "or face the consequences of your actions"?'

'As I told you, it's just a tactic,' Gaskell replied. 'If they don't pay up after that final letter, I get the debt collector involved, and you know what that means.'

'Yes,' Matthews replied. 'Mr Gaskell, did you ever meet Mr Young, or was it only Mrs Young you had dealings with?'

'Just the wife.' Gaskell sighed, clearly boring of the conversation.

'Did Mrs Young ever tell you why she required this money from you?'

'She never told me.' Gaskell's voice quietened. 'Although, you do hear gossip.'

'Gossip?' Matthews pushed for more detail.

'Well, I can't be sure, but I did hear she would attend cocktail evenings with the ladies of higher class, and of course, they do enjoy a card game.'

'Are you saying Bess Young ran up gambling debts?'

'As I say, Detective, it was only rumours. I can't confirm her private affairs.'

'Of course. Thank you.' Matthews, who was still clutching the letter, stuffed it back into his trouser pocket.

'Is that everything, Detective?' Gaskell spoke abruptly. 'I'm a busy man and have things to do.'

Matthews narrowed his eyes, detecting a hint of defensiveness in Gaskell's response. 'We will be continuing our investigation on Bess Young's murder, Mr Gaskell. If we find any evidence linking you to it, you will be held accountable for your actions.'

Gaskell's facade faltered for a moment, and a

flicker of unease passed over his face. 'I have nothing to hide, Detective. You're welcome to search my premises if you believe it will prove my innocence.'

Matthews nodded, his gaze unwavering. 'We may take you up on that offer, Mr Gaskell. But for now, we will continue our inquiries and speak with others involved in this case.'

With a final nod, Matthews turned on his heel, signalling to Harvey that it was time to leave. Determined to uncover the truth, he and Harvey headed back to the station, ready to delve deeper into the investigation that had taken them to Gaskell's door.

***

Detective Matthews entered his office, his mind occupied by the latest developments in the Bess Young case. To his surprise, he found Clara Blackwell waiting patiently in the worn leather armchair.

'Miss Blackwell,' Matthews said with an air of surprise. 'What brings you here today?'

Clara leaned forward, her voice eager yet measured. 'Detective, I believe I may have found something relevant to the investigation. I stumbled upon this discarded bag near the theatre.' She gestured to a small bag, which she had placed on Matthews' desk. 'And upon closer inspection, I'm convinced it belongs to Alice Grey.'

The detective's interest was piqued. 'What makes you think it belongs to Miss Grey?'

Clara reached into the satchel and pulled out a pair of black satin gloves, a delicate silver pendant, and a half-burnt letter. She placed them on the desk in front of Matthews, who leaned in for a closer look.

'These items were hidden away in the dustbins, but they caught my eye,' Clara explained. 'The gloves have a distinct style, matching the ones Alice used to wear during Victor Crown's performances. The pendant bears a unique engraving, which I believe could be a significant clue. And this letter, although partially burnt, seems to have been written by Alice herself. There are also a few other items of clothing inside, but these are the ones that stood out to me.'

Matthews examined the items carefully before emptying the contents of the bag across his desk to search through the remaining items. 'This is valuable evidence, Clara. We must determine why these items were discarded.'

As Matthews continued to inspect the items, Harvey couldn't help but interject. 'Miss Blackwell, how did you find these?'

'I was searching for any clues around the theatre,' Clara replied with a broad smile. 'I'd already checked around The White Horse and Griffin, where Miss Grey had been staying, but I didn't find anything around there.'

'We too had a look around the narrow alleys and dustbins,' Matthews interjected. 'So these items must have been placed in the theatre dustbins only recently. However, I must say that although we appreciate your help, searching through bins isn't your job. You're a journalist. Leave the detective work to the professionals.'

Clara raised an eyebrow, her tone dripping with sarcasm. 'Well, Detective, considering how many leads I've dug up compared to you, I might want to consider a career change.'

Matthews scowled before taking a deep breath. 'When did you say you found these items?'

'Just this morning, before first light.'

'Interesting,' Matthews rubbed his chin. 'I have had officers checking bins and alleys every day since the murder and there has been nothing at the theatre until now.'

Clara's eyes sparkled with excitement as she leaned forward, her voice laced with curiosity. 'What could that possibly mean?' She was undeniably thrilled to be actively engaged in the case.

'Well.' Matthews looked up from the pile of clothing. 'Either Alice Grey has returned to the theatre and discarded her belongings there, or somebody else threw them out on her behalf. No matter, my wife and I are headed to the theatre this evening, so we will be able to speak with Victor and his manager about this.'

As Matthews returned to carefully picking through the contents of the bag, Harvey, ever curious, couldn't resist questioning Clara. 'Miss Blackwell, may I ask you a question?'

Clara turned her attention to Harvey, a warm smile gracing her lips. 'Of course. What would you like to know?'

'Well, I couldn't help but wonder how you came to be a reporter. You seem so passionate about it, and it's rare to see a female reporter.'

Matthews glanced up to see Clara's reaction to the question, fearful that Harvey may have offended her, but to his relief, Clara looked more than happy to answer him.

Clara smiled warmly at Harvey's question, her eyes briefly glancing at the floor as if remembering her past. 'Well, Harvey, it all started when I was an orphan in Whitby. I was taken in by the kind-hearted wife of one of the Whitby Gazette editors. She provided me with a room and encouraged my passion for writing. I would often accompany my new father figure to the office, and I fell in love with it. As a child, I would write stories with the hope that one day, I would be able to get my own stories in the paper. A couple of years ago, they started paying me to proofread, and then last year, I submitted an article, which they decided to run. Since then, I've worked hard to keep myself writing pieces for the paper, and they seem to like what I submit.'

Her voice carried a touch of nostalgia, and

Harvey listened intently, captivated by her story. Matthews leaned back in his chair, intrigued by this unexpected revelation about Clara's past, trying to restrain himself from commenting on how these articles had included such negative ones about him.

'I learned the ropes of journalism through the Gazette, covering local events and stories. Over time, I realised the power of words and the importance of seeking the truth. It became my calling to uncover hidden secrets and shed light on the darkest corners of our town,' Clara explained, her voice steady and determined. 'It wasn't until this case, however, that I realised my work could also help your work.'

Matthews nodded, acknowledging Clara's dedication and the skills she had honed as a journalist. 'Your dedication to your craft is admirable, Miss Blackwell.' Matthews spoke through gritted teeth. 'Even if sometimes those articles put certain people in a negative light.' He wasn't going to say anything, but in the moment, he couldn't stop himself.

'I never meant to offend you, Detective.' Clara's expression conveyed genuine remorse. 'My stories about you and all the other high-ranking members of the town were supposed to be seen to make those in charge do better for the town. But now I've gotten to know you and the work you do, I appreciate how hard you work. Your position is through your own merit and not because of your father.'

'Thank you, Miss Blackwell.' Matthews smirked. 'I'm pleased our interactions have been positive.'

'Oh, please, call me Clara.' She smiled. 'Miss Blackwell makes me sound like an English teacher.' She gave a little snort as she laughed.

'Does your writing always involve investigating?' asked Harvey.

'To a degree, yes.' Clara smiled. 'I enjoy researching and investigating, but it's not always crimes and scandals I write about.'

'How so?' Harvey quizzed.

'Well, I am currently writing a piece about Isabella Bird. Have you heard of her?' Harvey shook his head. Clara continued, 'Isabella became the first woman to be awarded Honorary Fellowship of the Royal Scottish Geographical Society in 1890, and this month, she was finally allowed to become the first woman to officially join the society. It's a huge achievement for women, and so I'm an admirer of her.'

'I look forward to reading the completed article,' Matthews interjected before returning his gaze to the items on his desk once more, recognising their significance. 'Just returning conversation to the case, Clara, your discoveries could be crucial. We must delve deeper into the connection between Alice Grey, Victor Crown, and the events surrounding Bess's death. I appreciate your dedication and willingness to help, and I'd like you to keep helping us until this case is put to bed.'

CHAPTER 16

Detective Matthews and his wife emerged from their home, their steps filled with a shared anticipation. Grace's arm was looped through her husband's, her fingers entwined with his as they walked side by side to the carriage that awaited them. It was already dark outside, and the warm glow of the gas lamps flickered along the cobbled streets as they made their way to the theatre, anticipation buzzing in the air.

Matthews wore a smart dinner suit, with a perfectly fitted tailcoat with a cutaway front and split tail to the rear, featuring silk lapels. Underneath, he wore a pristine white shirt with gold cufflinks and a waistcoat of deep reds and golden detailing. To complete the outfit, a black bowtie, which had taken Matthews forever to tie as it was rare he wore one.

Grace, who wore a dress matching the colour of her husband's waistcoat, looked stylish in her floor-length gown with a voluminous skirt, creating an elegant silhouette. Her blonde hair was styled into a sophisticated all-up look, and her delicate gold earrings and pendant necklace added a touch of sparkle and refinement.

As they approached, they could see the theatre was lit up. Perched on the dark cliff side, it looked as though it was hovering, as if Victor Crown had already begun his illusions. The sound of the waves crashing beyond was the only indication of the sea below them. Harvey, who had gone ahead early to keep watch out for anything suspicious, was waiting eagerly for their arrival, and greeted them with a warm smile.

'You look beautiful, Mrs Matthews.'

'Thank you, Harvey.' She beamed at the sight of him. 'You're looking smart yourself.' Harvey too was wearing an evening dinner suit, although at short notice, they'd had to find him one of

Matthews' old ones from his youth. The fit wasn't perfect, but he did look suave, despite his usual unruly hair.

Together, they stepped into the bustling lobby, filled with the buzz of anticipation for the evening's performance. As Matthews scanned the crowd, his eyes met the gaze of the theatre manager, Mr Thomas Archer, who was out greeting people as they arrived. Recognising the detective instantly, Mr Archer hurriedly made his way towards them, his face etched with concern.

'Detective Matthews.' Mr Archer greeted him with a sweaty handshake, his voice carrying a hint of worry. 'Is this visit related to the investigation?'

Matthews nodded, his gaze focused. 'Indeed. I am here to enjoy the evening's performance with my wife, but I also need to speak to a few key witnesses before the night is over. One of them is your barmaid, Martha Bell. It's imperative that I gather more information from her regarding the case.'

Mr Archer furrowed his brow. 'I'm sorry, Detective, but we don't have anyone named Martha Bell working here. Are you sure you have the right name?'

Matthews exchanged a glance with Harvey, a flicker of confusion passing between them. 'I spoke with a Miss Martha Bell in my office just a few days ago. She claimed to be the one to discover the body of Bess Young on her way home. Are you certain she's not on staff?'

Mr Archer shook his head firmly. 'Detective, I assure you, there is no Martha Bell employed here. We have a small and close-knit team, and I know each member by name. Perhaps there has been a misunderstanding.'

Matthews felt a tinge of frustration rise within him, but he remained composed. 'I see. Thank you for clarifying, Mr Archer. I must have been misinformed.'

Grace interjected, her voice filled with curiosity. 'Darling, could it be that Martha Bell used a different name through fear of being found out by the killer?'

'Interesting idea, Mrs Matthews,' Mr Archer replied. 'I can ask all of the staff to wait behind after this evening's performance, Detective. If one of them did use the false name of Martha Bell, then I'm sure you will recognise her, yes?'

'Thank you, Mr Archer.' Matthews shook his hand again and led Grace on through the lobby. As they made their way deeper into the theatre, Grace reached out and gently squeezed Matthews' hand, offering a comforting presence. Harvey, always observant, piped up with a suggestion.

'Would you like me to speak with the theatre staff during the performance? They should be quiet while the show is on.'

Distracted by a man in the corner, Matthews didn't hear Harvey's suggestion. 'Grace, you go on through and find our seats with Harvey. I just need to speak with somebody first.' He planted a soft kiss on her cheek and swiftly manoeuvered through the crowd of people who were gradually proceeding into the auditorium. Sitting on a stool in the corner sat Harry Denton, Victor Crown's manager.

'Excuse me, Mr Denton,' the detective called, and Mr Denton visibly rolled his eyes at the sight of Matthews. 'May I have a quick word?'

'What can I help you with this time, Detective?' He greeted Matthews with a hint of weariness in his voice, his demeanour clearly indicating he was not inclined to engage in conversation.

'A bag was attained earlier today from the dustbins behind the theatre, with items inside that I believe belonged to Alice Grey.'

'And?' Denton replied, downing the last dregs of his drink.

'Do you know anything about these?'

'She left many things at the theatre, Detective, and as a manager it is also my responsibility to ensure the theatre is left clean and tidy upon our departure. It may only be Tuesday, and our last show is Friday, but I would prefer to throw out our rubbish as we go along rather than wait until the end.'

'You consider Miss Grey's belongings worthy of the dustbin?'

'Nobody has heard from her in days, and quite frankly, I don't have time to decide what is valuable and what is not.'

'Did you inform Victor that you were disposing of her belongings?'

'What does he care?'

'Well, she is his assistant. Maybe there are items he would want to keep.'

'Such as?'

'The gloves and other outfits that she performs in, perhaps.'

'If Victor decides to get himself a new assistant, I'm sure he would be happy to get a new set of gloves, Detective.' Denton stood and was now face to face with Matthews. 'Now, if there's nothing else, Victor will need me backstage before the show begins.'

'I will require speaking with Victor again this evening,' Matthews interjected before Denton left.

'The show is about to start, detective. You can speak to him another time.'

Matthews didn't say another word and watched as Harry Denton let himself through a door marked "Staff Only". There was something about that man he simply didn't trust.

CHAPTER 17

The dim lights of the theatre cast a hushed ambiance over the audience as Matthews and Grace settled into their seats, accompanied by Harvey. Anticipation hung in the air, palpable and electrifying. They were eager to witness the magic and illusion that awaited them as the curtain prepared to rise.

'Did you manage to speak to Victor?' Harvey whispered over to Matthews.

'Not yet,' Matthews replied, keeping his eyes focused on the stage that was now being revealed by the raising curtain.

As a small orchestra played a melodious overture,

the atmosphere crackled with excitement. Suddenly, a spotlight illuminated the centre of the empty stage, and with a crackle and small explosion of smoke, Victor Crown appeared, a figure cloaked in mystery and intrigue. The audience erupted into applause and murmurs of delight at his sudden appearance.

Dressed in a tailored black suit with a crisp white shirt and a shimmering red silk cravat, he exuded an aura of mystery and confidence. His presence alone commanded attention, capturing the gaze of every spectator in the theatre who was watching him in silent awe.

With a flourish of his hands, Victor began his performance, showcasing a series of sleight of hand tricks and mind-boggling illusions. His nimble fingers moved with precision, making cards vanish and reappear, coins float in mid-air, and objects seemingly teleport from one place to another. Gasps of astonishment and murmurs of wonder rippled through the crowd as Victor effortlessly manipulated reality before their very eyes.

As the show progressed, Victor's charisma and showmanship shone through. He captivated the audience not only with his incredible illusions but also with his engaging stage presence and magnetic charm. Grace leaned in closer to her husband, her eyes wide with amazement and delight. 'Isn't he something?' she whispered.

Matthews, ever observant and analytical, couldn't help but study Victor's every move, searching for clues and insights into the performer's craft. He marvelled at the seamless execution of each trick, admiring the masterful misdirection and the careful orchestration of the illusions. Yet, in the back of his mind, he couldn't shake the lingering questions surrounding the mysterious death of Bess Young and the possible connections to the enigmatic Victor Crown.

With a theatrical sweep of his arm, Victor extended his gaze out to the audience, scanning the sea of faces before him. His eyes landed on a young woman seated near the front, her eyes wide with anticipation. 'You, my dear,' he said, pointing directly at her. 'Would you do me the honour of joining me on stage?'

Gasps and whispers swept through the audience as the woman's face flushed with a mix of excitement and apprehension. She nodded, rising from her seat, her heart pounding with anticipation. Grace nudged her husband, her eyes sparkling with excitement as they watched the scene unfold.

As the young woman made her way to the stage, Victor greeted her with a warm smile, extending his hand to guide her to his side. 'What is your name, my dear?' he asked, projecting his voice so the entire audience could hear.

'Emily,' she replied, her voice quivering with a mixture of nervousness and exhilaration.

'Welcome, Emily.' Victor spoke with reassurance. 'Now, please, I want you to inspect this box.' He presented a small wooden box to her, allowing her to examine it thoroughly. 'Make sure it's empty and there are no hidden compartments. You are the eyes of the entire audience now.'

Emily, careful not to miss any detail, examined the box with great diligence. The audience watched intently, fully engaged in the unfolding spectacle.

Satisfied with her inspection, Emily handed the box back to Victor, who took it with a flourish. 'Thank you, Emily,' he said, acknowledging her contribution. Within seconds of returning the box to Victor, he reopened it to reveal a parchment inside. Emily gasped at the sight of this sudden appearance. Victor took out the parchment and handed it to Emily. 'Please read this aloud,' he instructed her.

'I, Victor Crown,' Emily spoke, her hands shaking with nerves, 'would like to thank Miss Emily for being my glamorous assistant during this trick.' The audience gasped at the mention of her name before erupting into applause.

'Would you like Emily to help me with another trick?' he asked the audience, who immediately cheered. Victor then returned his gaze to Emily. 'Now, if you would please step into this cabinet.'

A beautifully crafted wooden cabinet was pushed onto the stage by two ushers. It was adorned with intricate carvings and shimmered with an air of mystery. Emily hesitated for a moment, her eyes darting between Victor and the cabinet. She took a deep breath, summoning her courage, and stepped inside.

As Emily positioned herself within the cabinet, Victor closed the doors, effectively concealing her from view. He waved his hands dramatically in the air, incanting a few mystical words, and then, with a swift motion, he opened the cabinet doors once again.

To the astonishment of the audience, Emily had vanished. The space where she stood was now empty, the cabinet revealing nothing but emptiness.

Gasps of disbelief filled the theatre as the audience tried to comprehend the impossibility of the feat they had just witnessed. Whispers of excitement and bewildered awe spread throughout the crowd.

'I believe this is the trick that Bess Young was a part of,' Harvey whispered to the detective.

Matthews leaned forward in his seat, his eyes fixed on the stage, determined to unravel the secrets behind Victor's illusions. His analytical mind worked overtime, trying to decipher the mechanics and misdirection at play.

With a flourish, Victor closed the cabinet doors, signalling the completion of his illusion. A moment of suspense hung in the air as the audience awaited Emily's reappearance.

Victor swung the door open once more, and there stood Emily, unharmed and wearing an expression of sheer astonishment. The theatre erupted in applause, the crowd rising to their feet in thunderous appreciation for the extraordinary display of magic.

Victor graciously took a bow, his eyes gleaming with satisfaction. He beckoned for Emily to join him at the centre of the stage, giving her a warm embrace as the audience's applause filled the air.

As the theatre settled down, Detective Matthews and Grace exchanged astonished glances, their minds racing to comprehend the bewildering illusion they had just witnessed.

Once the audience had gone silent, Victor moved to the edge of the stage and began slowly and quietly walking down the steps towards the audience. Tension and anticipation flooded the crowd as they waited to see what Victor Crown was about to do next.

'Ladies and gentlemen,' Victor proclaimed, his voice resonating through the theatre. 'For my next illusion, I require a brave volunteer. Someone who possesses both beauty and courage. And I believe I have found the perfect candidate.' He extended a hand past Harvey, who was seated on the end of the aisle, and towards Grace.

'No.' Matthews grabbed a hold of Victor's hand and tried to remove it from his wife's arm.

'It's okay.' Grace turned and looked at her husband. 'I would like to do it.' Feeling the eyes of the audience on him, Matthews let go of Victor's hand and watched with unease as he guided Grace up onto the stage, his stomach in knots before anything had even begun.

Victor led Grace to the centre of the stage, where his eyes locked with hers. 'Are you ready for an extraordinary journey, my dear?' he asked, his voice laced with excitement and caution. Grace, eyes wide, nodded.

Victor then took Grace to the side of the stage where he whispered instructions to her quietly, ensuring that none of the audience could hear what was going to happen. As they spoke in private, the ushers began pushing on a towering structure made of steel and glass, an intricate web of contraptions and pulleys. It loomed over the stage, casting an intimidating shadow.

'This, ladies and gentlemen,' Victor announced, 'is the Vault of Shadows. Within its depths lies a challenge like no other.'

The audience held its breath, their eyes fixed on the stage as Victor explained the perilous nature of the illusion. Matthews felt a chill run down his spine as he absorbed the magnitude of the danger that awaited his wife.

'Grace,' Victor said, his voice filled with both gravity and reassurance, 'You will enter the Vault of Shadows. I will wrap chains around your ankles and wrists and secure these with padlocks. I will close and lock the door behind you, plunging you into absolute darkness. Your task will be to navigate the labyrinth within and find the keys that will unlock both your chains and your escape.'

Gasps of awe and concern echoed throughout the theatre, but Grace remained composed, her faith in Victor unwavering.

'However,' Victor continued, his voice now deeper with a more dramatic tone, 'you have only four minutes to escape, otherwise the hanging shards of glass and steel suspended above you and the vault will come crashing down, destroying the vault and all within.'

Matthews could barely contain his fear, but he knew he had to trust both his wife's judgment and

Victor's expertise. He clenched his fists, his eyes never leaving Grace's form as she stepped into the Vault of Shadows.

Victor began wrapping the chains around Grace, securing them with a lock. He allowed the audience one final look at her before the doors of the vault closed with a resounding thud, engulfing Grace in complete darkness. Matthews leaned forward in his seat, his heart pounding in his chest.

'Time starts now!' shouted Victor as he turned over a large hourglass, which he positioned on a small table at the side of the stage.

Victor then began working with precision and skill, manipulating the mechanisms and pulleys that controlled the chamber and the hanging glass and steel above it, which were now swaying slightly and looking ever more dangerous. The audience watched in awe as the Vault of Shadows came alive, its gears whirring, and the faint sounds of Grace's chains echoing through the theatre.

Minutes felt like an eternity, each passing second amplifying the tension within the theatre. Matthews could barely breathe, his eyes fixed on the vault, desperately awaiting Grace's emergence.

Matthews' eyes darted between the sand within the hourglass and the contraption that imprisoned his wife, his palms sweating as the sand began to run out. Grace had still yet to appear.

Suddenly, a blinding light erupted from the Vault of Shadows, causing Matthews to momentarily shield his eyes. The audience gasped as the large shards of glass and steel collapsed onto the vault in an almighty crash. The audience gasped, with numerous ladies screaming in horror. Matthews was on his feet without realising it, his mouth gaping open at the sight of the destroyed staging before him.

Victor Crown walked into the centre of the stage, and before anybody could speak, he pointed to the back of the auditorium. Grace walked down the centre aisle, triumphant and unharmed, clutching a small set of keys in her hand. The crowd erupted into thunderous applause, their cheers and exclamations reverberating through the theatre.

Victor beamed with pride, taking Grace's hand and leading her back up onto the stage to share in the audience's adulation. Matthews felt a wave of relief wash over him, his admiration for both

Grace's bravery and Victor's mastery of illusion intertwining.

As the applause gradually subsided, Detective Matthews couldn't help but join the audience in honouring the astonishing performance. The realisation that Grace had emerged unscathed from such a perilous feat filled him with a profound sense of gratitude.

He applauded not only for the artistry of Victor Crown but also for the unwavering spirit and resilience of his beloved wife.

As Grace re-joined Matthews in the audience, her face flushed with exhilaration, he enveloped her in a tight embrace. 'Are you all right?' he whispered, concern lacing his words.

She nodded, a radiant smile gracing her lips. 'I'm fine, darling. It was thrilling, truly. Victor knows what he's doing.'

As the applause subsided, Victor took a bow, his eyes gleaming with satisfaction. The curtain fell, signalling the end of the performance. The theatre buzzed with excitement and wonder, and Detective Matthews couldn't help but marvel at the magic that had unfolded before his eyes.

CHAPTER 18

Detective Matthews and Grace stood together outside the theatre, the cool night air providing a refreshing respite after the exhilarating performance they had just witnessed, within the warm stuffy auditorium. They conversed animatedly about the awe-inspiring illusions they had observed, dissecting the intricacies of Victor Crown's show.

'I didn't think for a moment that I would be up on stage with Victor Crown.' Grace giggled like a school girl. Matthews had not been at all impressed with Victor choosing his wife, and he just knew Victor had done so simply to humiliate him. Yet, he also had to admit that this had been the first time he had seen Grace so happy in a long time.

'You were wonderful up there.' He placed his arm around her, worried she may have been getting cold from the strong wind coming off the North Sea. The audience was slowly dispersing, and the entrance to the theatre where they stood was still loud from the hustle and bustle of everybody leaving.

As they waited for Harvey to return with the carriage, a familiar figure brushed past Matthews in a hurry to leave. It was Harry Denton. He clearly hadn't noticed the detective among the rest of the crowd. He briskly walked onto the street and out of view.

'Detective Matthews,' called out a voice laced with urgency. Matthews turned to see Clara Blackwell walking towards him.

'Clara?' Matthews frowned as the young reporter squeezed her way through the crowd.

'I have information you need to hear, and it cannot wait,' she said upon reaching the detective's side.

Matthews and Grace turned their attention to

Clara, their curiosity piqued. They exchanged a glance before Matthews took his wife by the arm and led her and Clara away from the theatre entrance to an area where they could speak more freely. 'What have you discovered, Clara? Is it about Victor Crown?'

Clara took a moment to catch her breath, then handed over an envelope to the detective. She spoke in hushed tones, aware of the sensitive nature of their conversation. 'I've been digging deeper into Victor Crown's past, and I've uncovered some intriguing links.'

Matthews immediately opened the envelope and read the contents to himself.

'How did you...?' Matthews' eyes narrowed, his mind racing as he contemplated what he had read.

'Just doing my job, Detective,' Clara smiled. 'I told you that I too can find out information my own way.'

Matthews took a deep breath, a sense of determination settling over him. 'Thank you, Clara, for bringing this to my attention. I had intended on speaking with Victor this evening before tonight's performance but didn't manage to. However, with this extra information, I think it would be foolish of me to wait until tomorrow.'

Just then, the sound of approaching hooves caught their attention. Harvey appeared around the corner, leading a horse-drawn carriage towards them. His eyes widened with curiosity as he noticed Clara in their midst.

'Harvey,' Matthews called out, his voice carrying a sense of urgency. 'I must ask you to escort Grace home. I need to go back into the theatre to speak with Mr Crown.'

'Right away, Detective.' Harvey held out his hand to help Grace into the carriage, his gaze momentarily flickering to Clara, who he looked at with a scowl.

Grace settled into the carriage, the dim light from the streetlamp casting a soft glow on her face. She looked at Matthews through the open window, her eyes filled with disappointment.

'Grace,' he began gently. 'There's something urgent I need to discuss with Victor. I promise I won't be long, and I'll be home as soon as I can.'

He reached out to touch her hand through the open window, his eyes filled with reassurance. She gave a subtle nod, but he could tell her frustration. With Clara by his side, they watched as the carriage pulled away from the theatre.

'Follow me,' Matthews told Clara as he turned on his heels and made for the theatre once more.

'What? Surely you don't need me,' Clara replied, scurrying to keep up with Matthews' longer strides. 'You want to help, then stick with me.'

Detective Matthews made his way back through the lobby, which was now much quieter, and let himself through a side door to the backstage area. He walked briskly through the backstage corridors of the theatre until he approached Victor Crown's dressing room and knocked loudly on the door. Victor, who was removing his stage costume, appeared at the door within seconds, his brow furrowed with concentration. His countenance displayed an unmistakable lack of enthusiasm upon spotting Matthews standing there.

'Detective,' Victor greeted, his tone polite but guarded. 'To what do I owe this unexpected visit to my dressing room again?'

'Mr Crown, may we have a word with you?' Matthews asked, his tone both firm and respectful.

Victor glanced up, his gaze meeting Matthews' with curiosity and caution before looking at Clara with a puzzled expression. 'Of course, Detective. Come on in.'

The dressing room was just as dark and cramped as Matthews remembered it from his last visit. 'If this is about your wife, Detective, then please do not lecture me. I am not in the mood for your husbandly concerns.'

'This is not about my wife, Mr Crown, though for the record, it was pretty clear why you chose my wife. I am not interested in playing games with you.' Victor smirked, amused that he had gotten under the detective's skin, just as he had hoped. 'Then why are you here?'

'I've recently come across some information concerning your personal life, Mr Crown,' he began, his voice steady. 'Specifically, allegations made by your wife regarding infidelity and violence. Care to explain?'

Victor's eyes widened for a moment before a mask of composure settled back over his face. 'Ah, the rumours and whispers.' He sighed, a tinge of resignation colouring his voice. 'With all due respect, Detective, I'm not sure what my personal problems have to do with you.'

'When you are a suspect in a murder investigation, everything is important to me.' Matthews stood firm. Clara stood in awe, having never seen this side of Matthews.

Victor hesitated for a moment before dropping himself onto the small wooden seat in front of his dressing table. 'My wife and I have been having difficulties for some time now. The strain of my career and never being home, the allure of adoring fans, and all the letters that arrived... it can take a toll on a marriage. Though nothing illegal about that, a lot of marriages struggle and end in separation these days.'

Matthews observed Victor's subtle gestures, searching for any signs of deception. 'And what about the accusations of violence, Mr Crown? Can you explain those?'

Victor's shoulders slumped, resignation and regret shadowing his features. 'I admit, Detective, that our arguments have sometimes escalated beyond control. But violence? No, never. I would never lay a hand on my wife or anyone else. It saddens me that she feels the need to say that just to guarantee a divorce.'

The detective's gaze remained unwavering. 'Mr Crown, may I remind you that these allegations from your wife will not help your defence as a suspect in the murder of Bess Young.'

Victor's expression softened, a flicker of vulnerability crossing his eyes. 'I understand your duty, Detective.'

'Mr Crown, can you also tell me about your arrest in Edinburgh six months ago?'

'Erm…' Clara leaned in and whispered to Matthews. 'That wasn't in the report I handed you.'

'No, Clara. Believe it or not, I also do my own investigative work too.' Matthews spoke but remained looking at Victor, his tone harsher than he had intended.

'Edinburgh was an accident.'

'You were arrested for causing life-changing harm to somebody.'

'He was a member of the public. I told him to stay still for the trick and he didn't.' Crown's voice rose as he tried to defend himself.

'That was not the only reason you were arrested,

though, was it, Mr Crown?'

'No.' Victor pursed his lips.

'After the same show, you were arrested for attacking somebody in the street.'

'They jumped me! I was merely defending myself.'

'By causing a gentleman to be covered in his own blood?'

Victor, his face etched with lines of distress, was clearly rattled by this conversation. 'You seem to be missing out the fact, Detective, that I too was covered in my blood. The man burst my lip and gave me a bloody nose and a cut above my eye.'

'Was this gentleman related to the person who was injured during the show?'

'Yes.' Victor sighed. 'Although I only learned of that afterwards.'

'You were charged?'

'I was given a record for causing injury to the man on stage, and I paid a fine.' Victor's face flushed with humiliation, and he couldn't meet Matthews' gaze, his eyes dropping to the ground as he clenched his fists in frustration. 'I have also been banned from returning to that Edinburgh theatre.'

A heavy silence filled the room as the weight of the conversation settled between them. Victor's gaze shifted, his eyes tracing the patterns of the carpeted floor. 'Detective, I must implore you to tread carefully. These accusations, they can destroy not only my career but also the illusion I've worked so hard to maintain.'

'The illusion?'

'I am a performer, Detective. The man you see on stage is very different from the man off-stage. It is an act, and one I have worked hard at perfecting. It has gotten me where I am today.'

The detective's gaze softened, a touch of empathy shining through. 'Rest assured, Mr Crown, I am committed to seeking the truth. The true essence of justice lies in uncovering the facts, regardless of their implications. If you have nothing to hide, then you have nothing to fear.'

Victor nodded, with gratitude and uncertainty in his eyes. 'I understand, Detective.'

'Before we leave, Mr Crown, can I ask if you've had any correspondence with Alice Grey?'

'None at all.' Victor sighed. 'I thought she would've returned by now. She has more than likely returned to London.'

'I saw your manager leaving in a hurry just now.' Matthews leaned against a nearby table, his demeanour slightly relaxed. 'Any idea where he could be headed with such haste?'

'Well, I just fired him, so, hopefully, far away.'

'Why did you fire him?'

'It's been something I've considered for some time now.'

'Any particular reason?'

'I don't believe he has my best interests at heart any longer. He had been trying to get me to fire Alice, and I honestly think he was the one to send her away. He never liked her.'

'Had Alice done something to offend Mr Denton?'

'Well... erm.' Victor pursed his lips as he considered the question.

'Mr Crown, the first time I spoke with your manager, he insinuated that you were having a more intimate relationship with Alice Grey, is this true?'

'Yes.'

'I see.' Matthews mused, glancing at his pocket watch in the dimly lit room. 'Perhaps that sheds some light on his feelings towards her. It's time for us to go, but I anticipate our paths will cross again in the coming week.

With that, Detective Matthews and Clara turned to leave the dressing room, leaving Victor Crown with his thoughts. As Matthews stepped back into the backstage corridors, his mind churned with the weight of the investigation.

'Why did you bring me back there for that?' Clara asked. 'I didn't do anything but stand there.'

'Whether you like it or not, you have gotten yourself involved in this investigation, and I think it's time you had a front row seat.'

CHAPTER 19

WEDNESDAY 30TH NOVEMBER 1892

The early morning sunlight cast a warm glow through the windows of the Matthews' home, filling the rooms with a sense of tranquillity. Detective Matthews stood in front of the long narrow mirror in the hallway, adjusting his tie with precision. He glanced over at Grace, who was putting on her coat and adjusting her hat in front of the door.

Grace's cheerful demeanour provided a respite from the intensity of Matthews' work, serving as a reminder of the love and normalcy that anchored him. He had been pleased to see that her positive mood from the previous night had continued into the morning, and he was hopeful that this was the beginning of a new chapter after what had been months of heartache.

'Ben, have you seen my gloves?' Grace called out, her voice carrying a hint of playfulness. Matthews retreated to the bedroom, his attention on the small task at hand. Returning a couple of minutes later, he said, 'They were on the dressing table.' He offered a gentle smile as he handed them over.

As Grace took her gloves, Matthews leaned in to kiss her, his presence a comforting reassurance. 'I'll be heading to the office shortly. If you like, Harvey can give you a lift in the carriage. He should be here soon.'

Grace nodded, slipping her gloves onto her delicate hands. 'Oh, I'm not going to work until later today. I'm heading to see Charlotte this morning. I'm sorry, I thought I told you. She's been eager to see me since I got back into town, and I've missed little Hugo.'

'Ah, well, do send my love to my sister, and Hugo, of course,' He wrapped his arms around her and gently kissed her on the lips. 'Enjoy your catch-up without me,' he teased.

Grace leaned into his touch, appreciating the solace it provided. 'I will, Ben.' She smirked. 'Thank you.'

With a final exchange of affectionate glances, they gathered their belongings and made their way out of the door. Matthews escorted Grace to their shared carriage, helping her settle in before joining her. Harvey, who was sitting up front, gave his usual 'Good morning' to them both.

As they journeyed through the cobbled streets, the early morning sun lit up the sky in bright reds and oranges, a beautiful contrast to the dark sea. The carriage ride to Charlotte's house was short, yet Grace still managed to cram in a conversation about the Victor Crown show, and how excited she had been to be on the stage.

Matthews listened intently, his mind finding solace in her upbeat voice. The drive passed in a blur, and soon, they arrived outside Charlotte's house.

'Here we are,' Matthews announced as the carriage came to a gentle stop. He turned to Grace, his eyes filled with affection. 'Enjoy your visit, my love. I'll see you this evening.'

Grace leaned over, planting a soft kiss on Matthews' cheek. 'Thank you, Ben. I'll see you tonight. Take care, and remember to eat.' She knew what he was like when it came to working. He would often forget to stop for any kind of break or even to eat and drink if he was too distracted.

He nodded, gratitude swelling within him for her unwavering support. 'I will, Grace. You take care too.'

With a final exchange of farewells, Grace alighted from the carriage, the sound of her footsteps receding as she made her way to Charlotte's front door. Matthews watched her go, a mix of pride and longing coursing through him as the carriage took him in the direction of the police station.

Grace gave the door a loud bang with the large brass door knocker and waited, her anticipation of a joyful visit quickly turning into worry as she received no response. She knocked again, and still no answer. She suddenly heard the faint sound of baby's cries drifting through the closed door, heightening her concern.

'Charlotte?' she called, hitting the wooden door with her fist. Nothing. Grace's heart quickened with concern as she stood outside. She tried to lean across and look through the front window, but she couldn't reach.

With a sense of urgency, Grace reached into her purse and retrieved a spare key, which she had been given for emergencies. She hesitated for a moment, hoping that everything was all right before inserting the key into the lock and pushing the heavy door open.

As she stepped into the house, baby Hugo's cries grew louder, echoing through the silent rooms. Grace followed the sound, her heart pounding with anxiety and apprehension. She found Hugo in his small crib in the centre of the master bedroom, his tiny face scrunched up and tears streaming down his cheeks.

Rushing to his side, Grace gently lifted him into her arms, cradling him with tenderness. 'Shh. It's all right, little one,' she murmured, her voice soothing. 'Aunty Grace is here now.'

As she comforted the distressed baby, her eyes scanned the room, searching for any sign of Charlotte. Her gaze fell upon a figure huddled in the corner on the floor, shoulders shaking with silent sobs.

'Charlotte?' Grace called out softly, her voice filled with concern.

Charlotte looked up, her tear-stained face revealing both anguish and relief. 'Grace,' she whispered, her voice trembling. 'I... I didn't know what to do. He's been crying for hours, and I just couldn't... I couldn't...'

Grace's heart went out to her sister-in-law. Though Grace had not yet experienced the challenges of motherhood, she understood that at times it must be difficult. She approached Charlotte, with baby Hugo still in her arms, and sat beside her on the floor. Charlotte gently wrapped her arms around her, leaning her head on Grace's shoulder as she looked down at her red-faced baby boy in the arms of his auntie.

'It's okay,' Grace reassured her sister-in-law, her voice soothing. 'You're not alone. I'm here now. Let's figure this out together.'

Charlotte clung to Grace, her body shaking with a mixture of exhaustion and emotional strain. Grace was more than happy to be there for her, offering silent support and understanding.

After a few minutes, Charlotte's tears gradually ceased, and she cast a tired smile towards Grace. 'Thank you,' she whispered, her voice resonating with profound appreciation.

Grace returned the smile, her eyes filled with compassion. 'Of course, Charlotte. We're family. You should have come to me if you were struggling.'

'I didn't think I could.' Charlotte sniffled.

'Why ever not?'

'Well, you've not exactly had the easiest of times lately either.'

'Oh, Charlotte. Don't for a moment think that my miscarriage could ever take me away from wanting to help you and Hugo.' She squeezed Charlotte's hand.

Together, they settled baby Hugo, tending to his needs and eventually soothing him back to sleep. With the immediate crisis resolved, Grace and Charlotte took a seat at the end of the large double bed, watching over the sleeping baby. They spoke of the challenges of pregnancy, motherhood, the overwhelming responsibility, and the fear of not living up to expectations.

Charlotte opened up to Grace about her struggles as a mother, how she was finding it difficult to do even the simplest of tasks, and how she felt as though she wasn't bonding with her baby. In return, Grace spoke about her own feelings about her miscarriage, and her worries about trying again.

In that moment of vulnerability, the two women felt as though the weight of their worries was a little lighter. They had each other, and Grace realized they were not alone in their fears and that having that support from one another was crucial.

'Where's John?' asked Grace.

'At work.'

'Is he aware of your struggles?'

'A little. He doesn't know how to help me.' She sighed. 'Although, I don't know how to help me either.'

'Sometimes you just need a little break.' Grace squeezed her hand again. 'From now on I will come over on the days I'm not working, and we can either spend the time together and talk about whatever is on our minds, or if you need some alone time, then I can look after Hugo for you.'

'I can't ask you to do that.'

'You didn't need to ask. I want to spend more time with you both. Plus, it's important you have some you time.'

As the morning continued, Grace and Charlotte relocated to the living room, where they enjoyed hot drinks as Hugo continued to sleep. Their connection and deepening conversation grew stronger with each passing hour. In the midst of their challenges, they found solace in one another and the unwavering love that bound them together.

Once Charlotte felt more relaxed, she began talking about other things, including asking Grace about the Victor Crown show. Grace was giddy as she told Charlotte all about the show, and Charlotte could hardly believe it when Grace told her about going on stage.

'I bet my brother was beside himself.' Charlotte laughed.

'He didn't look too impressed, that's for sure.'

'I'm surprised he didn't try and put a stop to it.'

'Oh, he tried.' Grace giggled. 'But I told him I wanted to do it.'

'So, how did you end up at the back of the auditorium?'

'Goodness, is that the time?' Grace sniggered as she stood up.

'Oh, no. You have to tell me!'

'I couldn't possibly reveal Victor's secrets. But honestly, I do have to leave for work.'

'I'll get it out of you,' Charlotte teased as she walked Grace to the front door.

'I'll call in again this evening on my way home, and tomorrow, I'm not working, so I'll come around to spend the day with you both unless you already have plans.'

'Not at all.' Charlotte smiled. 'We will be thrilled to have you.'

CHAPTER 20

WEDNESDAY 30TH NOVEMBER 1892

Matthews slumped into his office chair, the weight of the case resting heavily upon his shoulders. The room was dimly lit, the only illumination provided by the flickering flame of a single oil lamp. Across from him, Harvey sat with an air of seriousness, his young face etched with determination as he looked down on the evidence and multiple pieces of paper with Matthews' handwriting all over them.

They had been sat in silence now for what felt like an eternity, reading and re-reading the notes in front of them. Matthews rubbed his temples, feeling the exhaustion seep into his bones. He had spent countless hours poring over evidence, speaking to witnesses, and connecting the intricate threads of the investigation. Yet, something eluded him, a missing piece of the puzzle that lingered just beyond his grasp.

Just as frustration threatened to consume him, a knock on the door interrupted his thoughts. He glanced at Harvey, who nodded in understanding. Matthews rose from his chair and opened the door to find Clara Blackwell standing in the hallway, her gaze focused and determined.

'Detective Matthews,' Clara greeted, her voice laced with urgency. 'You wanted to see me?'

Matthews nodded. 'Thank you for coming, Clara. I thought it would be beneficial for us to discuss the case, to pool our knowledge and insights.'

Clara nodded and entered the office, closing the creaky door behind her. She smiled at Harvey, acknowledging his presence, but it was clear from the expression on his face that Harvey was less than happy to see her. The last time he had seen her she was heading off to question Victor Crown with Matthews, and Harvey was starting to think that she was looking to take his job.

'Please, take a seat.' Matthews gestured at the empty seat next to Harvey, his gaze fixed on the papers scattered across his desk. 'Clara, I'm glad you could join us. We've been going through the evidence and analysing every lead we have. But I can't shake the feeling that there's something we're missing. That's where I think you may be of use. You see things from a different angle and you have a sharp eye. I would value your opinion.'

'Thank you, Detective.' Clara settled into the chair, her gaze fixed on Matthews. Her notebook was at the ready, her pen poised to capture any important information. 'I understand your frustration. Sometimes, an outsider's perspective can shed light on overlooked aspects. Let's review the case together.'

Matthews leaned back in his chair, his exhaustion evident in the lines etched on his forehead. 'We have Victor Crown, a skilled illusionist with a troubled personal life. There are accusations of infidelity and violence, but we need more concrete evidence if we are to accuse him. We also have the financial troubles of Bess Young, the threatening letters, and the possible connection to Charles

Henry Gaskell, the loan shark.'

'Do you still think he's a suspect?' Harvey asked.

'Everyone is still a suspect at this point,' Matthews replied.

'Why is he a suspect?' Clara asked.

'He sent Mrs Young threatening letters only days before she died. He claims that she paid the debt and that he has no interest in her anymore. But where did she suddenly get the money from, that's what I want to know.'

Clara scribbled on her notepad. 'So, do you think her payment could have been made with her life?'

'It's not the first time I've seen that happen.' Matthews shrugged.

'What about Alice Grey?' Harvey asked. 'Surely, her disappearance is suspicious.'

'She was and still is a suspect.' Matthews nodded. 'But her disappearance is also a concern to me. Victor is convinced that she has returned to London, and if that's the case, then we need to find out whether her guilt has led her to flee or if somebody else has driven her away.'

'What about Victor's manager?' Clara interjected. 'Harry Denton clearly didn't like Alice.'

'True.' Matthews sighed. 'But disliking your client's assistant because they are sleeping together doesn't give us a good enough reason why Bess Young would be murdered. I can't see the connection. Although, we do need to find him today. If Victor really has fired him, we need to make sure he doesn't skip town while the investigation is ongoing.'

'Then, of course, we have Bess's husband and sister,' Harvey pointed out.

'The husband is certainly keeping something from us,' Matthews said.

'How do you know that?' asked Clara.

'I've interviewed enough criminals to be able to see the tells.' Matthews grinned. 'It's like poker. You just have to figure out the players' tells, and Mr Young is more obvious than anyone when it comes to trying to cover up his lies. I just need him to slip up.'

'And what of Miss Metcalf?'

'She is still a person of interest.' Matthews scanned the table and pulled out the paper connected to her interview. 'It's clear she has feelings for Mr Young, and there's resentment towards her sister because Timothy refused to leave her for him.'

Clara scribbled notes furiously, her eyes darting between Matthews and Harvey. 'These are all crucial angles to consider. But what's the next move?'

Matthews rubbed his eyes and leaned over his desk, scanning the papers that littered it. 'We need to speak to Harry Denton,' Matthews finally said. 'If he has been fired, then I want to see him again before he tries to leave town. I think he knows more about Alice Grey's whereabouts than he is letting on. There have been no trains out of Whitby since I saw him leave the theatre last night, so it's unlikely he'll have left yet.'

'I can head on down to the station to look out for him,' Harvey suggested.

'And I can go to the White Horse and Griffin to see if he is still there,' Clara replied.

'There is, of course, another part of the puzzle I have yet to tell you.' Matthews spoke slowly, his mind skipping backwards and forwards.

'What's that?' Harvey replied after a short pause.

'Martha Bell.'

'Who?' Clara asked, puzzled.

'The morning after the body of Miss Young was discovered, a Miss Martha Bell arrived in my office. She claimed she was the one who discovered the body on her way home from the theatre, where she works, and had sent a young child to find me that night.'

'So, what does that have to do with anything?' Clara still looked baffled.

'When I asked the theatre manager last night if I could speak with Martha, he informed me that nobody with that name worked there. After you left, Clara, I stayed back to speak with the staff. I didn't get anything of use, and more importantly, I didn't see the woman claiming to be Martha Bell.'

'So whoever this woman was, she lied about her name?' Harvey asked.

'Possibly,' Matthews replied. 'But more importantly, she lied about working at the theatre.'

'Why would she do that?' Clara asked.

'I have two theories.' Matthews sighed. 'Either she has something to hide, or she's worried the real killer will find her.'

A knock on the door interrupted their conversation. Matthews raised an eyebrow, glancing towards the door. A young constable stood there, holding an envelope in his hand.

'Detective Matthews, I was asked to deliver this to you,' the constable said, his voice respectful as he extended the envelope towards Matthews.

Matthews took the envelope and quickly recognised the handwriting on it. It was from Mr Waters, the coroner. With a sense of urgency, he tore it open and began to read. His eyes widened as the words etched on the paper sank in.

'Harvey, Clara,' Matthews began, his voice laced with a mixture of concern and curiosity. 'Change of plan.'

'What's happened?' Harvey couldn't hide his eagerness.

'An unsettling development has arisen,' Matthews began, his voice tinged with a sombre tone. 'The coroner, Mr Waters, has informed me that the body of a young woman has been found washed up on the shore. He suspects it may be Alice Grey.'

Clara's eyes widened, her hand flying to her mouth in shock. 'Alice? This could be a breakthrough. A tragic one.'

Harvey's face paled, the gravity of the situation

settling heavily upon him. 'We need to know for sure. It would explain why we've struggled to find her.'

The weight of the moment hung in the air, each of them grappling with the possibility of their worst fears being realized. Matthews took a steadying breath, his resolve firm.

'I will need both of your assistance this morning,' Matthews said.

'Of course,' Harvey and Clara replied in unison. They exchanged determined glances, their resolve mirroring that of their mentor.

Matthews offered a grateful smile, his confidence in his team swelling within him. 'Thank you. I need you to locate Victor Crown and Harry Denton.' Matthews stood and began gathering his belongings as he spoke. 'They're both staying at the White Horse and Griffin Inn, so start there. I won't personally be able to identify the body as I have never met Alice Grey, but either of them will,' Matthews continued, leading them all out of the office, along the corridor, and towards to entrance of the station. 'Escort them to Mr Waters' office as soon as you can.'

CHAPTER 21

WEDNESDAY 30TH NOVEMBER 1892

Detective Matthews stood in the dimly lit corridor of the coroner's office, his thoughts swirling with anticipation and apprehension. Mr Waters approached him, his gaze filled with sympathy and professional resolve.

'Detective, I appreciate your prompt arrival,' Mr Waters initiated, his tone carrying a solemn weight. 'The body has been prepared for identification. We must proceed with caution and sensitivity.'

Matthews nodded, his expression grave. 'Thank you, Mr Waters. Can you tell me about her discovery?'

'Not much to tell really,' Mr Waters told him as

he led the way. 'She was found washed up on the rock pools under the abbey cliff by a couple of kids.'

As they entered the examination room, the sterile scent of antiseptic filled the air. The body lay upon the wooden slab-like table, draped in a clean white sheet. Matthews steeled himself, ready to face the truth that lay beneath the fabric.

As they awaited the arrival of Harvey and Clara, Matthews engaged Mr Waters in a conversation about the forensic examination, seeking any preliminary insights that might assist in their investigation. The coroner, an older more fragile man these days, had decades of experience. With a methodical precision, he shared his observations, shedding light on the nature of the body's condition and the possible cause of death.

'I have only had a small amount of time to look at the body thus far,' Mr Waters said as he pulled back the sheet.

'Of course.' Matthews was unaffected by the revealing of the dead woman. 'I'm sure your full report will be as detailed as always.'

'Indeed.' Mr Waters shakily put on his large milk bottle-like glasses before continuing. 'If you look at her hands, wrists, neck, and torso, you can see very little to no bruising at all. This leads me to believe there was no struggle. Although, as you can see from the skin shrivelling, she had clearly been in the water for some time.'

'So, you would conclude that she died from drowning?'

'I would never conclude until I have done a full examination, but from first observations, that is my suspicion.'

'Did she arrive naked, or have you already removed her clothing?'

'She arrived completely naked.'

Matthews glanced at his watch, noting the time ticking by. He hoped Harvey and Clara had located Victor and his ex-manager. Mr Waters recovered the young woman's body and offered Matthews a drink in his office while they awaited the others.

Another half an hour passed and Matthews was starting to worry. What if Victor Crown and Harry Denton were being difficult and refusing to help? He couldn't just sit around waiting, and he got to his feet just as there was a knock on the office door.

Matthews leaned across and swung the door

open, revealing Harvey, his expression etched with strain and trepidation.

'Detective, Mr Waters,' Harvey greeted. 'We've brought both Victor Crown and Harry Denton. Clara is waiting with them outside.'

Matthews exchanged a glance with Mr Waters, their shared understanding propelling them forward. 'Thank you, Harvey. Please bring them in.'

Moments later, Clara walked up the corridor with Victor Crown and Harry Denton, both of whom looked alarmed at where they had been taken.

Matthews nodded, acknowledging their arrival. 'Thank you both for coming. This office is a little small, so let's proceed with the identification. Mr Waters, if you would.'

Mr Waters led the group into the examination room, where the draped figure lay upon the table. The room was bathed in an eerie light, casting elongated shadows on the walls, adding to the gravity of the moment.

'Harvey and Clara,' Matthews broke the silence. 'You are welcome to wait outside if you'd prefer. Seeing something like this is not for everyone.'

'I'm okay,' Clara quickly replied.

'Yeah… me too,' Harvey added.

Victor Crown, his face a mask of apprehension, approached the table with measured steps. Harry Denton dragged his feet behind and stood next to him at the table. The weight of the situation was palpable, the air thick with anticipation. Matthews observed closely, gauging Victor's and Harry's reaction, seeking any tell-tale signs that could provide insight.

Matthews took a step forward, his voice steady yet tinged with empathy. 'Gentlemen, we believe this may be Alice Grey. I need you to carefully observe the body and confirm her identity.'

Mr Waters stood by the head of the table, his gloved hands poised to unveil the body. Matthews took a steadying breath, his focus homing in on the task at hand.

'Mr Waters, proceed,' Matthews instructed, his voice steady.

The coroner nodded and slowly pulled back the white sheet, revealing the lifeless form beneath. The figure was eerily still, the pallor of death casting an unsettling aura. Victor and Harry glanced down, their gazes fixated on the body.

Victor's brow furrowed, his expression contorting with a mix of anguish and disbelief. 'No,' he whispered, his voice barely audible.

Harry Denton, his eyes widening in shock, seemed unable to tear his gaze away from the body. 'It's so difficult to tell. The body is so... so strange looking.'

'It's the effects of being in the water for so long,' Mr Waters explained.

'This is not Alice.' Victor sighed. A mix of relief and sorrow washed over him.

'You are certain?' Matthews replied.

'Absolutely,' Victor replied and took a step back from the table. 'Alice was much shorter than this woman, and her hair was shorter and a bright ginger.'

'Well, if you're sure, I thank you for your time.' Matthews leaned over to shake the men's hands in turn before ushering them towards the door.

'Come on, Harry.' Victor sighed. 'Let's go.'

'How dare you speak to me as though nothing has happened.' Victor and Harry stood face to face in the starkly lit corridor outside the examination room. The tension between them crackled in the air, their emotions running high after the unsettling identification process. Detective Matthews observed them closely, sensing the brewing storm of conflict.

'I beg your pardon?' Victor raised his voice to match that of his ex-manager.

'You have the audacity to ignore me the entire walk to this place, and once it's clear it isn't Alice, you speak to me as though everything is all right? You fired me, Victor!' Harry's voice seethed with indignation. 'After all these years of loyalty and dedication, this is how you treat me?'

Victor's face contorted with frustration, his voice sharp and defensive. 'Don't act innocent, Harry. You know why I had to let you go. Your management decisions were jeopardizing the integrity of my career.'

Harry's brows furrowed, his voice tinged with bitterness. 'Jeopardizing your career? I've been your pillar of support all these years, Victor. And now, after everything, you accuse me of incompetence?'

Victor's voice rose, his anger unleashed. 'Incompetence? No, Harry. It's more than that. It's about Alice. I saw the way you looked at her, the way you manipulated her, using your position to exploit her vulnerability. I know you sent her away. You've been wanting me to fire her for long enough!'

Harry's face flushed with rage, his fists clenching at his sides. 'Exploit her? You're the one who took her under your wing, promising her a bright future! And as always, you ended up bedding her, like you do with all your assistants. You were so blind to her sexual exploits that you couldn't see she was undermining you at every turn. I am the one who has to clean up the mess when your assistants get hurt because you bore of them, moving onto a new assistant or sleeping with a fan instead. I may have told her to leave, but what does that say about your 'care' for her if she does so willingly?'

Victor's eyes blazed with fury, his voice filled with accusation. 'You dare to question my concern for Alice? You only saw her as a threat because she came up with some great ideas and you were worried that those ideas would see you out of a job.'

Harry took a step forward, his face inches from Victor's. 'Mark my words, Victor. You will regret firing me!'

Detective Matthews stepped forward, his

authoritative voice cutting through the heated exchange. 'Gentlemen, this is not the time nor the place for personal disputes. We must focus on finding the truth and bringing justice to the situation at hand. I ask you both to quietly return to the White Horse and Griffin and remain there until this investigation comes to an end.'

'Detective, I am due to leave at the end of the week,' Victor said. 'I am due to perform in Harrogate from the end of next week.'

'Well, let us pray we resolve this in time.' Matthews sighed. 'But I'm afraid until we have put this case to bed, I will need you both to remain in Whitby. Do I make myself clear?' Victor and Harry both nodded through pursed lips.

A tense silence descended upon the corridor as the two men locked eyes, the weight of their fractured partnership hanging heavily in the air. The echoes of their argument reverberated within the walls, a stark reminder of the deeper tensions that fuelled their dynamic.

As they all turned to leave, they were suddenly brought to a halt by Mr Waters' voice from behind them. 'Excuse me, gentlemen. Would you mind coming back into the examination room for me?'

Matthews led Victor and Harry back into the room, with Harvey and Clara trailing behind.

'Is there something else, Mr Waters?' Matthews asked.

'Well, possibly.' Mr Waters gestured for them to follow him into a colder room with several bodies lined up, all covered with the same crisp white sheets.

'What is this?' Victor's brows furrowed with genuine concern, his eyes reflecting a mix of worry and unease as he scanned the room.

'Mr Crown, when you identified the young woman out there not to be Alice Grey, you told me a little about what she really looks like.' Mr Waters put on a pair of gloves and invited them towards another covered body. 'I thought it was worth you looking at another body I have, just in case.' A heavy silence enveloped the room.

Mr Waters lifted back the sheet to reveal another young woman who had severe bruising to the arms, neck, and torso. A gasp escaped Victor. 'That's Alice!'

'Interesting.' Mr Waters directed his comment at

Matthews. 'Because this is the body that Timothy Young identified as being his wife, Bess Young.'

Matthews' eyes bulged with shock as the entire room fell into a stunned silence.

Chapter 22

As the coroner's office emptied, Harry Denton stormed out, his footsteps echoing with an air of frustration and resentment after his argument with Victor. Detective Matthews glanced at Victor Crown, whose face bore a mix of anguish and regret. Matthews knew he had to act quickly to prevent the situation from escalating further.

'Victor,' Matthews began, his hand gently resting on the illusionist's shoulder. 'I realise tensions are high, but it's crucial that you have a conversation with Harry. After your decision to let him go, he's expressed his intention to leave town. For now, it would be best if everyone stays put until we have a better grasp of the situation.'

Victor sighed, his shoulders slumping under the weight of the conflict. 'It's too late, Detective. I doubt he will listen to me; I don't think there's anything that can mend our relationship now. The damage has been done.'

Matthews locked eyes with Victor, his determination evident. 'Perhaps, but I fear Harry will skip town, and we can't afford to lose a key witness with everything that's transpired.'

'But he betrayed my trust,' Victor retorted, a hint of vulnerability creeping into his voice. 'He was supposed to manage my career, not interfere with my personal life. What am I supposed to do, fire him but ask him to stay in town for moral support?'

'I understand your quandary, Victor,' Matthews replied. 'But if either of you decided to leave town now, it would only serve to make you both look guiltier.'

Victor took a deep breath, contemplation etched across his features. 'All right, Detective. I'll talk to him. But I won't beg for him to stay. If he chooses to leave, I'll have to accept it.'

Matthews nodded in understanding. With newfound determination, Victor set off after Harry.

'What's the plan?' Harvey asked as he, Matthews, and Clara left the coroner's office together.

'I'm going to see Mr Young.' Matthews spoke in hushed tones as they walked together along the street. 'He's under arrest for the misidentification of Alice Grey's body and intentionally providing false information during a murder investigation. Harvey, I need you to return to the station and bring an officer and a carriage, just in case things turn nasty.'

'What about me?' Clara interjected. 'What can I do to help?'

Matthews had momentarily forgotten that Clara was still present, and a flicker of concern crossed his mind, knowing well the probing nature of her profession as a journalist. Had he let her in too much? The last thing he wanted was for her to go away and write an article about all this. So far, she hadn't written anything about the case, but he knew he still needed to be careful with her. 'Keep a watch on Victor and Harry,' Matthews replied. 'I want to know their movements, especially if Harry tries to flee town.'

The three of them bid each other farewell and headed off in different directions, determination on each of their faces.

Clara had the shortest journey and quickly found herself outside the White Horse and Griffin, where Victor Crown and his manager had been staying all week. Unwilling to stand out in the cold for goodness knew how long, Clara walked into the bar area to discover it was deserted. It was a little early for drinkers, so the landlord was more than likely in the back somewhere. Not wanting to be caught, Clara quickly darted for the narrow staircase and cautiously began to climb to the upper floors.

With a determination to uncover the truth, she found herself outside Victor Crown and Harry Denton's rooms, their muffled voices alerting her to their location. The soft glow of candlelight spilled from the partially closed door, casting eerie shadows in the dimly lit corridor.

As Clara inched closer, her heart pounded with both excitement and trepidation. She pressed her ear against the door, listening to the voices within.

'Harry, I need to know the truth.' Victor's voice carried a mix of accusation and desperation. 'Did you have anything to do with Alice's death?'

Harry's response was sharp, his tone indignant. 'Of course not! I would never harm her, or anyone for that matter. Have we not known each other long enough for you to know I could never do something like that?'

Clara's curiosity intensified, and she resisted the urge to push the door open just a bit more. She was determined to capture every word, every emotion that unfolded in this crucial conversation.

Victor's voice quivered with emotion. 'But you made it blatantly clear you disliked her. It wasn't so long ago you were telling me to fire her! The way you looked at her with disgust... It all makes me wonder.'

A moment of tense silence followed, and Clara could almost sense the charged atmosphere in the room. Then, Harry's voice softened, carrying a hint of remorse.

'You're right, Victor. I didn't like her. She had gotten far too big for her boots, and she clearly thought she was the one running the show. I'm not an idiot. I can see how she manipulated you. I just wish you could see through her deceit as clearly as I do.'

'You always had a way of ruining things.' Victor's voice was laced with exasperation and accusation. 'You couldn't stand that Alice was more than just my assistant. She was like family to me, and you resented her for it.'

Harry's retort was biting, his voice filled with pent-up frustration. 'Family, you say? A woman you were having an affair with while she was just an employee? She had no business acting so high and mighty when her position was beneath you.'

'That's not fair!' Victor's deep voice rose with indignation. 'Alice had talent and potential beyond being a mere assistant. She had dreams, and I believed in her.'

'You always put her above everything and everyone else,' Harry shot back, his tone dripping with resentment. 'She had you wrapped around her little finger, and she knew you would've done anything for her.'

'Of course I would!' Victor's voice cracked with emotion. 'She was important to me, and I won't apologize for caring about her.'

'You know, Victor, I wouldn't be surprised if you

had something to do with her death. With those relentless reporters constantly lurking about, ready to unearth your affair, it's clear you couldn't stomach the idea of your reputation being tarnished once more.'

'That's absurd!' Victor's voice trembled with disbelief. 'I would never harm Alice. She meant too much to me.'

Clara's heart pounded in her chest. The accusation was shocking, and she wondered if Harry's words were borne out of anger or if there was a deeper truth behind them.

'Get out of my way, Victor,' Harry demanded. 'As I am no longer your manager, I have no reason to be here anymore, so I'm going home.'

'You're making a mistake, Harry.' Victor's voice was tinged with concern. 'Leaving town now will only make you look guilty. You have to stay and face the questions. Clear your name if you have nothing to hide.'

'And why should I trust you? You've fired me, accused me of things I didn't do, and now you want me to stay and face the consequences? More like you want me to help you keep your name clean in all this mess. You have no idea how to manage yourself, or the press, and you are finally realising how much I actually do for you.'

'I didn't want it to come to this.' Victor sighed, his anger subsiding into weariness. 'But I had to let you go, Harry. Your actions were becoming a liability to both of us. I can't risk my career for you anymore.'

Clara could barely hear them over the sound of her own beating heart and the blood rushing through her veins as she comprehended the gravity of the situation. Matthews had asked Victor to talk to Harry, but this was not the kind of conversation he meant. Now, the dynamics between Victor and Harry were becoming more complex.

'My actions were becoming a liability?' Harry laughed. 'You truly have no idea how many times I have saved your arse over the years. Alice Grey was just one of many situations you got yourself into. Yes, I asked you to fire her, not because she wasn't talented, but because she was manipulative, and you couldn't see that. You were too busy thinking with your dick.'

'I resent that.'

'Then it appears we have no more to say. Now, let me leave.'

'Look, Harry, I understand why you might be angry and hurt. But leaving town now will only make you look guilty. If you truly had nothing to do with Alice's death, then stay and help us find out what happened to her.'

'And if I stay, what then?'

'We've been friends for a long time, Harry.' Victor spoke more gently now. 'Let's not end things like this. Stay the rest of the week, please. The coroner said that man misidentified Alice as his wife. We can help the detective to see he is the culprit.'

Clara heard the sound of a bag dropping to the floor, and the squeak of bed springs indicated that one of them had taken a seat on the bed.

'Fine.' Harry's voice turned defeated. The room went quiet, and satisfied that Harry was no longer planning to flee town, Clara slowly crept away from the door, and as quietly as possible, made her way back downstairs and out of the White Horse and Griffin. She decided not to go far, just in case Harry had a sudden change of mind and decided to try and flee again

CHAPTER 23

WEDNESDAY 30TH NOVEMBER 1892

Harvey raced to the police station as quickly as his legs could carry him. Matthews had given him strict orders to get an officer and a carriage over to Timothy Young's house as soon as possible in case things turned nasty when Matthews confronted him about the incorrect identification of his wife's body.

The courtyard of the police station was bustling with activity as Harvey arrived, with stable hands cleaning out the horses and officers coming and going. His mind was focused on the task at hand when he noticed an unfamiliar carriage parked to the side. It wasn't one that belonged to the force. As he approached, he recognised Lady Graham standing beside it, a smile on her face.

'Harvey!' Lady Graham called out, stepping forward with her arms extended. 'I hope I'm not interrupting anything important.' She placed her gloved hands on his shoulders and greeted him like an old friend. 'I remembered you mentioning you worked here, so I thought it the best place to start looking for you.'

Surprise painted an unmistakable expression across Harvey's face, his eyes widening and his jaw dropping slightly as he processed his unanticipated visitor. 'Not at all, Lady Graham. It's just... unexpected to see you here.'

Lady Graham chuckled softly. 'I can imagine. I've come with someone who wishes to see you.' She gestured towards the carriage.

Harvey's heart skipped a beat as he recognised the man stepping out.

'George,' Harvey whispered, his voice tinged with surprise and hope. 'What...' But he couldn't get out his words.

George turned to face his younger brother, and Harvey saw a mixture of emotions in his eyes,

Surprise, uncertainty, and a hint of longing.

'I didn't expect to see you here,' Harvey finally spoke, trying to keep his emotions in check.

George shifted uncomfortably, clearly grappling with his feelings. 'I... I didn't know if I wanted to be here,' he admitted. 'When I saw you, I think I was just in a state of shock. I thought I had left everything in Whitby behind. I had no idea I had a younger brother.'

Harvey took a deep breath, trying to steady his nerves. He had waited for this moment for so long, and now it was finally here. 'I don't blame you for being angry or hurt. I just wish we had found each other sooner.'

George's gaze softened, and he looked at his brother with a mix of vulnerability and scepticism. 'It's not just about that,' he said quietly. 'I had my reasons for leaving Whitby, and I didn't want to be reminded of the past.'

'I understand. I won't pretend to know what you've been through or the reasons behind your decisions.'

The tension between the brothers began to dissipate, and Lady Graham watched with a small smile on her face. 'Sometimes, it takes time and understanding to heal old wounds,' she said softly. 'And having somebody there by your side who loves you can help you to heal.'

George glanced at Lady Graham, then back at Harvey. 'I suppose you're right,' he said, his voice tinged with emotion. 'I can't promise that everything will be easy, but... I'm willing to give this a chance. I have always wanted a family.'

'Does this mean you plan on staying in Whitby?' Harvey asked, trying not to sound too excited about the prospect.

'Well, I will need to find a place to stay.' George gave a hesitant smile.

'I know a place.' Harvey beamed with delight, no longer able to restrain himself. 'But first, please excuse me. I need to go into the station for a moment. The detective sent me here with a task and I almost forgot it for a moment.'

'Oh my goodness,' Lady Graham gasped. 'Please go. We don't want to delay anything.'

Harvey raced inside the station, and a couple of minutes later returned to the courtyard where Lady Graham was returning to her carriage.

'You're not leaving already?' Harvey asked, a concerned look on his face.

'Oh, good heavens, no.' Lady Graham chuckled. 'I have a friend who lives in Whitby, so I am staying with her for a couple of days before I return home.'

'If I may.' Harvey smiled. 'I would like to tell Mrs Matthews that you're in town. I'm sure she would love to see you.'

'That would be delightful, poppet.' Lady Graham chuckled. 'I'll arrange for a little get-together before I leave town.' She gave them both a wave as her carriage pulled out of the courtyard, leaving Harvey and George alone.

'Don't you have any belongings?' asked Harvey. George shook his head. 'No matter,' Harvey continued. 'Most of my clothing is made by Mrs Matthews. I'm sure she would be happy to make you something too.'

As the two brothers continued to talk in the middle of the courtyard, they were blissfully unaware of the busy officers and stable hands working around them.

It was only when Detective Matthews returned to the police station that Harvey snapped out of his bubble. Matthews spotted them immediately and was curious to know who Harvey engaged in an earnest conversation with. Curiosity piqued, he approached them, his footsteps echoing in the courtyard.

'Harvey, who's this?' Matthews asked as he came closer, giving a friendly smile to his assistant.

Harvey jumped, worried that Matthews would be angry with him for getting distracted from the case. 'Detective, this is my brother, George.'

Matthews extended his hand in greeting. 'Pleased to meet you, George. I'm happy to see you here in Whitby.'

George shook Matthews' hand with a slight smile. 'Nice to meet you too, Detective.'

Matthews observed the brothers standing side by side, noting the similarities and differences between them. It was evident that this reunion had a profound impact on Harvey, and he was glad to see his assistant finally reconnecting with his brother.

Harvey quickly filled Matthews in on his surprise guest, and Lady Graham, whom he had just missed out on meeting.

'I'm glad you two had the chance to catch up,'

Matthews said warmly. 'Where are you staying in Whitby?'

'Erm...' George hesitated and looked at his brother blankly.

'We have a spare room,' Matthews interjected. 'It's the one Harvey used to sleep in when he stayed with us if you need a place.'

George's face lit up with delight. He couldn't believe somebody who had never met him could be so generous with their hospitality.

Harvey nodded, a mixture of emotions crossing his face. 'That would be great, as long as Mrs Matthews doesn't mind.'

'Oh, Harvey, I'm sure Grace will be more than happy to offer George a place to stay.'

'Only until I can get somewhere more permanent.' George replied, a hesitant smile on his face.

'Of course.'

'Hold on a minute.' Harvey suddenly snapped back to remembering the case. 'I thought you were going to Mr Young's house to question him?'

'I was, but he's not at home or his workplace.'

'So, what now?'

Matthews frowned. 'I've got officers posted to keep an eye out for him. If he's spotted, they've been told to inform me immediately.'

Harvey nodded, acknowledging the plan. 'Do you think he's still in town?'

'Yes. I was able to see through the windows and it doesn't look like he's gone too far.' Matthews looked distracted as he spoke and pulled out his pocket watch to check the time. 'I have to head back inside the station for a moment, but you are free to spend the rest of the day with your brother. Take him to the house if you'd like. I'm sure you're both hungry.'

Harvey nodded. 'Send word if you need me back, Detective.'

Matthews made his way back inside the police station, his mind now fully focused on the case. The disappearance of Timothy Young added another layer of complexity to the investigation, and he knew that every moment counted in their pursuit of the truth. He was now starting to piece the puzzle together in his mind, and he knew the final clue was just around the corner.

CHAPTER 24

WEDNESDAY 30TH NOVEMBER 1892

lara Blackwell stood concealed in the shadow of a nearby doorway, her eyes trained on the entrance to The White Horse and Griffin. She was determined to keep an eye on the movements of Victor Crown and Harry Denton in the hopes of uncovering any crucial information for the ongoing investigation.

The late afternoon was cold, and a light drizzle had begun to fall, but Clara's determination to help uncover the truth propelled her forward. As a journalist, she couldn't resist the allure of a compelling story, and the mystery surrounding the illusionist and his dead assistant had captured her curiosity.

As she kept her focus on the entrance of the inn, Clara spotted Victor Crown walking out, followed immediately by Harry Denton. Her heart quickened, and she focused intently on their movements. She knew that this would have been roughly the time Victor would have started heading to the theatre ready for the evening's performance, but why would Harry be joining him? Victor fired him as his manager, so what would make him need to go out? Clara also found it strange that there was no carriage awaiting them, and instead, they took off along the street on foot.

As the two gentlemen began to walk down the cobbled road of Church Street, Clara stepped out from her concealed doorway and began to follow them at a safe distance, ensuring not to lose sight of them.

However, her covert watch was cut short when a familiar voice called out from behind her. 'Clara?' She turned to find one of the editors of the Whitby Gazette standing nearby, an annoyed expression on his face. But this was not any editor, it was the one who took her in as a child. Mr Samuel Kelly. The middle-aged newspaper editor exuded an air of authority, his salt-and-pepper hair neatly combed and his spectacles perched on the bridge of his nose. His clothes, though smart, were worn and dull, giving the appearance he had owned them for many years.

'Clara Blackwell, what on earth do you think you're doing?' he scolded, before seeing Victor Crown up ahead, walking towards the end of the street. 'I thought I made it clear that you were to stay away from this investigation.'

Clara straightened up, her eyes unyielding. 'I'm just trying to help, sir. The public has a right to know the truth about what happened.'

The editor sighed, clearly exasperated. 'I understand your zeal for a good story, but this is a sensitive matter, Clara. It's best left to the professionals, like Detective Matthews.'

'But I can assist him! I've already gathered some valuable information for him.'

The editor shook his head firmly. 'No. You're putting yourself in danger, and it could compromise the investigation. You're a reporter, not a detective. Now, I want you to go home and focus on other stories.'

Clara felt a surge of frustration welling up inside her. She knew Mr Kelly had good intentions, but she couldn't simply abandon her efforts to assist in the case.

'Detective Matthews is my friend. I want to help him,' Clara retorted, trying to stand her ground.

Mr Kelly sighed, his expression softening. 'I do not understand your loyalty, Clara. It wasn't so long ago you were writing negative things about this man. Now, all of a sudden, you are his friend? Do you seriously think you're helping him solve a case?' Samuel paused, realising Clara was no longer trying to fight back on this. 'Of course he will take your help. You're doing the leg work for him and making his job easier. He's using you, Clara.' Clara opened her mouth to fight back, but Mr Kelly cut her off again before she could speak. 'Go home. Now.'

Clara's shoulders slumped in frustration, but reluctantly, she nodded in agreement. 'All right,' she said, her voice tinged with disappointment.

'Good. I'll walk home with you,' Samuel replied, his tone softening slightly. 'We'll cover this investigation from an appropriate distance, and if there are any updates, we'll report them accordingly.'

Clara hesitated for a moment, torn between her desire to help and the need to respect the editor's authority. Ultimately, she knew she had to trust in the professionals handling the case and the integrity of the Whitby Gazette.

With a sigh, she turned away from the entrance to The White Horse and Griffin, feeling disappointment and regret. Victor and Harry were now out of sight, so following them was no longer an option anyway. She would just have to find another way to help Matthews.

***

The flickering candles in Detective Matthews' office cast eerie shadows on the walls as he sat alone, surrounded by the haunting darkness of the night. The weight of the case pressed heavily on his shoulders, and frustration gnawed at his mind like a relentless spectre.

The sound of rain tapping on the windowpane added to the melancholic ambiance, echoing his frustration as he pored over the notes scattered on his desk. Each piece of evidence seemed to be leading him to the same conclusions. But he knew there was still not enough evidence to prove his theory.

He rubbed his temples in weariness and yawned before rubbing his tired eyes. The silence in his office began to feel oppressive. A firm knock on his door jarred him from his thoughts. Startled, Matthews looked up to see another officer standing in the doorway.

'Detective, we've spotted Timothy Young returning home,' the officer informed him, dripping wet from the rain and breathless from running down the hallway.

At the mention of Timothy Young's name, a surge of adrenaline coursed through Matthews' veins. He quickly grabbed his coat, slipping it on as he rose from his desk.

'Where is he now?' Matthews asked, his voice firm with determination.

'He's just arrived at his residence. We're keeping an eye on him, waiting for your instructions.'

Without another word, Matthews bolted from his office, his footsteps echoing down the corridors of the police station. The rain outside had turned the cobbled streets into a glistening canvas, reflecting the dim glow of gas lamps that lined the thoroughfare.

He made his way swiftly through the deserted streets, guided by the faint glow of streetlights. The urgency of the moment lent wings to his feet, and before long, he arrived outside Timothy Young's residence.

Two officers stood discreetly nearby, their eyes trained on the house where Timothy had returned. Matthews approached them, keeping his voice low as he spoke with them.

'Detective,' the officer whispered, acknowledging Matthews' presence.

'Any sign of him?' Matthews asked, his voice barely above a whisper.

'He's inside, Detective. Looks like he's alone for now,' the officer replied.

'Stay alert, but don't approach until I give the signal. I want to speak with him alone first,' he commanded.

The officers acknowledged with nods, their professionalism shining through as they executed his commands without a moment's delay. Matthews inhaled deeply, preparing himself for the task at hand, walking off in large strides toward the front door.

As Matthews reached the threshold of Timothy Young's residence, his heart pounded with both apprehension and determination. He raised his hand and knocked firmly on the door, his senses heightened, unsure what mood he would find Mr Young in.

All of a sudden, there was a scurry of panicked movement from inside the house, and the sound of Timothy swearing from within. Without warning and before Matthews could react, the door swung open with force and Timothy stood there, his eyes wide with fear and anger, clutching a gun in his trembling hand. He pulled the trigger, causing an ear-piercing bang.

Matthews stumbled back in shock, the deafening sound echoing through the air. The bullet missed its intended target, whizzing past the detective's ear as the gun recoiled under Timothy's weak grip.

Realising the shot had missed, Timothy lunged at Matthews, their bodies colliding with force. The gun clattered to the floor, its danger momentarily neutralized. The two men grappled, each fighting for the upper hand. Timothy's desperation fuelled his actions, and he swung punches with reckless abandon, aiming to break free of Matthews' grip and flee.

With a surge of adrenaline, Timothy managed to break free, landing a powerful punch on Matthews' jaw with a force that sent the detective staggering backward.

Gritting his teeth against the pain, Matthews refused to back down. He knew he couldn't let Timothy escape; too much was at stake. As Timothy tried to make a break for it, the two officers on standby raced to Matthews' assistance.

'Stop! Police!' one of the officers shouted, his voice commanding authority.

Timothy tried to swerve the first officer, his fists ready to lash out again. The officers lunged at Timothy, successfully restraining his flailing arms. Despite his struggles, Timothy was outnumbered and soon found himself pinned against the wall, his escape thwarted.

Matthews, slightly bruised but undeterred, caught his breath as he looked at the man he had pursued for answers. 'Timothy Young, you are hereby under arrest in connection with the murder of Alice Grey and for providing false testimony in a homicide investigation,' he declared, his voice firm.

Timothy's eyes darted around, desperation flickering in their depths. 'I didn't do anything,' he protested, his voice shaky.

As they led Timothy away in handcuffs, Matthews couldn't help but feel a sense of relief. The dangerous encounter had ended without further harm, and Timothy Young was now in police custody, where he could be questioned. As the rain continued to fall outside, washing away the tension of the night, Detective Matthews knew the investigation was far from over.

CHAPTER 25

THURSDAY 1ST DECEMBER 1892

The faint light of a single candle gently illuminated the bedroom as Detective Matthews quietly dressed. It was early, and he was trying to be as quiet as possible to ensure he didn't wake Grace. His mind was already consumed by the case, the weight of it bearing down on his shoulders.

Just as he finished buttoning his shirt, a creak in the floorboards caused him to freeze. He heard a soft rustle of bedsheets behind him. Turning, he saw Grace stirring awake. Her eyes blinked sleepily as she propped herself up on one elbow.

'Benjamin, why are you up so early?' she asked,

her voice laced with concern.

Matthews turned to her with a gentle smile, though his eyes betrayed the weight of the ongoing investigation. 'I have to interview Timothy Young this morning. He's been in a cell all night, and I need to get some answers from him.'

Grace reached out and gently touched his arm, her concern evident. 'Do you think he'll talk?'

Matthews sighed. 'I don't know. Now, go back to sleep.'

Grace closed her eyes, but they sprang open again as another thought came to her. 'What about George?'

'What about him?' Matthews halted before reaching the bedroom door.

'He's in the spare room. What am I to do with him today?'

'I told him yesterday that the farrier is looking for a new apprentice, and that if he was interested to come to the station later today as he'll be there shoeing the force's horses.' Matthews walked back to the bed and kissed Grace on the forehead. 'Tell him to come down if he's still interested, okay?'

'Okay.' Grace yawned. 'Oh, also…'

'Yes?'

'I'm seeing Charlotte today. I was thinking I would invite her to pick out a Christmas tree with us.'

'Surely not yet?' Matthews appeared utterly appalled by the mere suggestion, his brows furrowing deeply, and his eyes widening in disbelief as he contemplated the notion.

'No, no.' Grace smirked. 'I was going to invite her today, but for us to do it in a couple of weeks.'

'Gosh, is it really that close already?' Matthews sighed. 'Summer was only two minutes ago.'

***

Detective Matthews entered the dimly lit police cells, his footsteps echoing off the cold stone walls. The cells, which were in the basement of the police station, were not designed for comfort, with a smell of damp and urine, and the bars turning rusty and black. The cold morning did very little to help the conditions; there was no heating at all. He approached the cell where Timothy Young sat, his face shadowed and unyielding. The events of the previous night were still fresh in Matthews' mind, not to mention the large bruise across his face from where Timothy had punched him.

'Good morning, Mr Young,' Matthews greeted, his voice calm and composed.

Timothy glanced up, but his expression remained stoic. He offered no response, choosing instead to maintain a stony silence.

'I need to ask you some questions about Alice Grey and Bess Young,' Matthews continued, trying to gauge Timothy's reaction.

Still, there was no response. Timothy sat with his arms folded, his eyes fixed on some distant point on the wall. It was clear he had no intention of cooperating.

Matthews took a deep breath, his patience wearing thin. He understood that the man before him was likely scared and defensive, but his lack of cooperation was hindering the investigation.

'Mr Young, you have the right to remain silent, but I must remind you that this is your time to tell me your side of the story,' Matthews said, hoping to elicit some reaction from the man.

Timothy's jaw tightened, but he said nothing.

'You're connected to both Alice and Bess,' Matthews pressed on, his voice firm. 'I need to know what happened to them.'

But still, Timothy remained stubbornly silent.

Matthews took a deep breath, trying to find a different approach. 'This morning, I have Victor Crown and his manager, Harry Denton, coming in to testify against you,' he lied.

Timothy's gaze flickered for a moment, but he quickly reverted to his blank expression.

With a sigh, Matthews turned to leave the cell. 'Think about it, Mr Young. I'll be back later. We can continue this conversation then.'

'I can't talk about it,' Timothy finally murmured, his voice barely audible.

'I understand that this is difficult for you, Mr Young. But withholding information won't help anyone, including yourself.'

Timothy shook his head, a flicker of anger crossing his features. 'I don't know anything. I was just arguing with Bess outside the theatre that night, and then she was gone.'

'Mr Young, why did you identify the body of Alice Grey as that of your wife?'

Timothy looked away again, a battle of emotions playing out on his face. 'I didn't hurt her,' he finally whispered, his voice strained.

'Mr Young,' Matthews continued, his voice measured but firm. 'Where is Beatrice Young. Where is your wife?'

Timothy hesitated, his eyes darting away for a moment before returning to meet Matthews' gaze. 'I don't know,' he replied, his voice barely above a whisper.

'Mr Young, I need to know if anyone asked you to lie about the identity of the body found in the alley,' Matthews inquired, his eyes focused on Timothy.

Timothy hesitated, his hands trembling as he clasped them tightly in his lap. He swallowed hard, as if trying to find the strength to speak. 'No one asked me to lie,' he finally replied, his voice barely above a whisper. 'But…'

'Yes…' Matthews pushed.

'Bess was not supposed to get on the stage with Victor,' Timothy muttered almost to himself. A faint frown crossed his face.

Matthews leaned forward, seizing upon Timothy's unintended statement. 'What do you mean by that? Why wasn't Bess supposed to be on the stage?'

Timothy's eyes widened, and he stammered, realizing his slip of the tongue. 'I... I meant... she shouldn't have volunteered to go onto the stage. It caused nothing but trouble.'

Matthews narrowed his eyes, his instincts telling him that Timothy was trying to backtrack. 'That's not what you said, Mr. Young,' he pressed. 'You specifically mentioned that she wasn't supposed to get on stage with Victor. What aren't you telling me?'

Timothy's face contorted in panic as he struggled to come up with an explanation. He knew he had made a grave mistake with his choice of words, and he was now entangled in a web of contradictions. 'I... I misspoke, Detective,' he stammered, wiping sweat from his forehead. 'You're twisting my words.'

Matthews watched Timothy carefully, his gaze unwavering. He could tell he wasn't going to get any more from him now. But unbeknown to Timothy, he had revealed to Matthews much more than he had realised.

Matthews thanked Mr Young and turned to leave, climbing the stone steps in a hurry. He quickly made it to the front desk, where he told the on-duty officer to have a carriage ready for him as soon as possible.

Detective Matthews hurriedly crossed the police station courtyard, his mind racing after his conversation with Timothy. Without hesitation, Matthews headed to the small accommodation above the stables where Harvey lived. He ascended the stairs two at a time and let himself into the room, finding Harvey already awake and alert.

'Harvey, we need to leave immediately,' Matthews said, his voice urgent. 'Something's come up, and we can't waste any time.'

Harvey looked surprised but didn't question the detective's urgency. He knew that when Matthews spoke with such urgency, it meant they were on the cusp of a crucial breakthrough in the case.

'Where are we going, sir?' Harvey asked, quickly getting out of bed and dressing as fast as he could.

'I'll explain on the way,' Matthews replied. 'Just get ready as quickly as you can. We don't have much time.' As Harvey dressed, Matthews told him about the events of the previous night and the arrest of Timothy Young.

'I was going to ask who gave you that bruise.' Harvey grinned. 'Thought Mrs Matthews had been boxing with you.'

Matthews chuckled at the thought. 'I haven't had a chance to share with you my discovery about Timothy Young losing his job either.'

'What?' Harvey exclaimed. 'When? How did you find that out?'

'I learned it yesterday,' Matthews replied as he ushered Harvey out of the door.

As they made their way out of the accommodation, Matthews quickly filled Harvey in on the final pieces of evidence he had generated, and that he was ready to close this case once and for all.

Back in the courtyard, a carriage with two horses was waiting for them. They wasted no time, racing through the streets of Whitby. The morning sun was beginning to cast a golden glow over the town, but there was no time to appreciate its beauty.

They pulled up outside The White Horse and Griffin, and without waiting, Matthews burst out of the carriage and through the inn's front door. He raced through the deserted bar area and up the wooden stairs. He already knew which rooms Victor and Harry occupied, and he began banging on them both simultaneously.

'What the bloody hell?' came Victor's voice. 'Who is it?'

'It's Detective Matthews.' He spoke with a serious tone. 'I demand these doors are opened immediately.'

Victor appeared at his door within seconds looking shocked and exhausted, dressed in a long nightshirt. 'What the hell is going on here?'

'Mr Crown, I require you and Mr Denton at the station immediately.'

'For goodness sake. Could this not have waited until a more reasonable hour?'

'I couldn't risk waiting,' Matthews replied as he again pounded his fist against Harry Denton's closed door. 'When did you last see your manager?'

'Last night.' Victor scowled. 'He was at the theatre with me, and we returned here together after the show. You told me to keep him around, and what better way than at the theatre?'

Matthews tried the closed door and was surprised to find it unlocked. Walking inside, he could see immediately that the room had been emptied.

'He's gone!' Matthews shouted as he raced back out of the room. 'Mr Crown, get dressed. I need you to be at the station in my office as soon as possible.' Victor nodded, looking more concerned now. Matthews then turned and raced down the staircase, where he bumped into the landlord at the bottom.

'Detective?' Mr Walker said with disbelief. 'What brings you here so early?'

'Harry Denton.' Matthews spoke with heavy breath. 'Do you know when he left and where he was going?'

'He got a carriage to take him to the train station ready for the first train out this morning.'

Matthews pulled out his pocket watch. It was quarter to seven, just fifteen minutes until the first train of the day was due to leave. Matthews raced back outside and ordered Harvey to get them to the station as quickly as he could.

A relatively short journey, the horses' hooves sounded loud as they echoed along Church Street. As they reached the train station, Matthews could hear the sound of the approaching train as they pulled up outside the entrance of Whitby train station. Matthews sprinted through the bustling crowd. With every stride, he pushed himself harder, his heart pounding in his chest. He could see the platform up ahead, and the train's whistle pierced the air, signalling its imminent departure.

As he reached the platform, Matthews caught sight of a familiar figure hurrying towards one of the train cars.

'Denton, stop!' Matthews shouted, his voice carrying through the station.

Harry glanced back, his eyes widening in surprise at the sight of the determined detective hot on his heels. For a moment, their eyes locked, and Matthews could see the flicker of panic in Harry's gaze.

Ignoring the curious gazes of other passengers, Matthews closed the distance between them. As adrenaline coursed through his veins, he extended his arm, seizing Harry's shoulder and prevented him from stepping onto the train, just as Harry's hand gripped the handrail of the train door.

'You're not going anywhere, Denton,' Matthews said firmly, his grip unyielding.

Harry struggled, attempting to break free. 'Let me

go! I have a right to leave if I want to!'

'Not when you're a person of interest in a murder investigation,' Matthews retorted. 'You have questions to answer.'

The train's engine roared to life, and the conductor's voice echoed over the platform, announcing the final boarding call. Time was running out, but Matthews wasn't about to let Harry escape justice.

Just as the train began to inch forward, Matthews knew he had to act quickly. He couldn't afford to let Harry slip through his fingers.

With a swift manoeuvre, Matthews spun Harry around and pulled him away from the train door, guiding him back towards the platform.

'Let's talk, Denton. There's a lot we need to clear up,' Matthews urged.

Seeing the train door slowly edging away from him, Harry hesitated, his shoulders slumping in defeat. The fight in him seemed to wane, and he finally relented, giving in to the reality that escape was not an option.

As the train pulled away from the platform, Detective Matthews led Harry back through the station, and out to where Harvey was waiting for them with the carriage.

Chapter 26

Thursday 1st December 1892

Detective Matthews paced back and forth across his office, his brow furrowed with deep concentration. The air was tense, heavy with anticipation, as Harvey stood silently in one corner of the room. Across from the detective's desk, Victor Crown and Harry Denton sat with a mixture of anxiety and curiosity etched on their faces. They exchanged occasional glances, unease evident in their expressions.

'Detective, may I ask what we're waiting for?' Victor finally asked, clearly frustrated at being made to wait.

'We are still waiting for one more person.'

Matthews spoke in a deep voice but didn't look at either of the men as he spoke.

Footsteps echoed in the corridor outside the office, growing louder as they approached. The door swung open, and Timothy Young was escorted into the room by two officers, his hands in handcuffs. His face was pale, his eyes darting between the occupants of the room. With no spare chairs, Timothy was left to stand next to the other men.

Matthews came to a stop, his gaze fixed on the men before him. 'Gentlemen,' he began, his voice steady, 'we are here to address the web of lies and secrets that have entangled us in this investigation. I am finally ready to reveal my findings.' Matthews took a deep breath before continuing. 'Mr Crown, Mr Denton, Mr Young, the truth always comes to light. For the sake of justice and the memory of those we've lost.'

He turned to Timothy, his gaze piercing. 'Mr Young, you've been a person of interest from the beginning. There's the infidelity to your wife with her sister, the public argument outside the theatre, and your clear inept ability to lie convincingly, not to mention trying to kill me last night with a pistol.

Then, of course, we have the fact that you deliberately lied when identifying the body of Alice Grey, and instead claimed it to be that of your wife.'

Timothy's jaw tightened, and he swallowed hard but didn't speak.

Matthews then turned his attention to Victor. 'Mr Crown, you have a history of violence, you are renowned for affairs with fans and you and Alice had a relationship that extended beyond the bounds of a traditional employer-employee dynamic. Due to your strained relationship with your manager, Harry Denton, you frequently chose to turn a blind eye to his misguided decisions, all in pursuit of a more harmonious working relationship. In exchange, you counted on him to handle the fallout from your public relations mishaps and any complications arising from your tumultuous affairs. You expected him to clean up your mess, but disliked him having an opinion or interfering with your personal affairs.'

Victor's eyes flickered, his fingers tapping rhythmically on his knee. Harry remained composed but alert, his eyes fixed on Matthews.

'And you, Mr Denton,' Matthews continued, locking eyes with Harry. 'From the moment we crossed paths, your inclination to maintain a considerable distance, not only from me but from the entire case, was evident. Your envy of Alice had left you disillusioned and embittered, and your need to control Victor led you to continuously seek opportunities to gain more money and power. At the coroner's office, your reaction to the young lady, initially considered to be Alice, was far from surprised when it was revealed not to be Alice. Yet the correct identification seemed to trigger an unexpected panic in you, prompting an attempt to flee town this very morning.'

Harry's jaw clenched.

'Now, let's address the truth,' Matthews declared, his voice commanding the room's attention as he finally sat in his chair behind the large oak desk. 'The victim we have been trying to find justice for all this time was Mrs Beatrice Young.' Matthews looked between the three men as he spoke. 'But recent events have taught us that Bess Young is not currently in the coroner's office, but the body of Alice Grey is. I therefore strongly believe that Bess Young is not dead at all.'

The revelation hung in the air, casting a weighty

silence over the room. Victor and Harry exchanged a glance, their surprise evident.

'You see, Mr Young,' Matthews continued, turning to Timothy, 'Bess Young's debts were growing, and the pressure was mounting. The threatening letters pushed her to the edge. You told me that you had no knowledge of these letters at the start of our investigation, and I confess you lie convincingly, but I was already aware that you knew about them before we found them in your home, as your sister-in-law informed me it was you who had talked to her about them before Bess's alleged murder.' Matthews paused for a moment. His eyes focused on the men intently before continuing. 'Ahead of your arrest yesterday, I came looking for you at your home and then at your place of employment, the council offices. I had an interesting talk with your boss, who informed me that you had been fired in recent weeks due to stealing the money you had been collecting, from the parish. Your intentions were to use this money to help pay off these debts, but it was not enough. So, when an offer to clear all those debts was made to the pair of you, it was an offer you couldn't refuse.'

Timothy shifted uncomfortably, avoiding eye contact, his face flushed pink.

Matthews continued. 'Alice Grey's death wasn't a mere coincidence. It was part of a sinister plot.' He took a momentary pause. 'Harry Denton, less than forty-eight hours after the murder, I saw you in The Plough Inn on Baxtergate, purchasing drugs from Charles Gaskell, who just so happens to be the debt collector of Bess Young. The first time I met you, you told me that you always arrive in a town a few days before Victor to ensure everything is set up. As a drug user, I would expect that you spent your first evening looking for somebody to supply you, and Charles Gaskell is never a difficult man to find for those looking to buy. Mr Denton, you asked Charles Gaskell for more than just drugs on your first meeting, and he denied you, but what he did do was tell you about a woman and her husband who might just be desperate enough to do anything for money. Mr Young, aware of your predicament, approached you with an offer. A promise to erase all your debts in exchange for a terrible deed. Timothy, you and your wife were drowning in debt, and your desperation clouded your judgment. Despite your infidelity towards your wife, you have always valued the vows of marriage and would stand by her until the end. This is also why you refused to reveal the whereabouts of your wife to me when I asked you in your cell. You think hiding her will protect her.'

Timothy's shoulders slumped, his guilt evident. Harry's jaw tightened, his eyes avoiding contact.

'A plan was hatched to murder Alice Grey,' Matthews continued, his gaze shifting between the men. 'Harry, Bess, and Timothy hatched a plan to conceal Alice Grey's murder and instead identify the body as Bess Young. You see, if the body was identified as Alice's, it would have been instantly associated with you, Victor, as well as Harry. It was easier for Harry to pretend he had sent Alice away.'

Victor's eyes widened in shock, his hand instinctively reaching for his chest. 'I had no idea...'

Matthews nodded, acknowledging Victor's surprise. 'Unfortunately for Mr Denton, his plan was derailed a matter of hours before the murder could take place, when you invited Bess Young onto the stage on that opening night, unintentionally linking Bess to the show. A decision that would forever link Victor Crown and Harry Denton to the murder of the presumed Bess Young. This was a mistake by Bess, who allowed herself to be overwhelmed by the invitation on stage, and it was also an unintentional lapse on your part, Mr Young, when you inadvertently revealed that this wasn't part of the original plan during our conversation in your cell.'

A heavy silence hung in the air as the reality of the situation settled on the three men. The intricate connections, the hidden alliances, and the sinister motives were finally laid bare.

'Of course, we soon came to realise that Bess Young was not the corpse, but instead, it was Alice Grey.' Matthews stood from his chair. 'In fact, I do believe I have met the real Bess Young.'

Timothy raised his head and looked at Matthews with bewilderment.

'Ah, yes.' Matthews tapped his chin. 'You see, Bess Young came to my office the morning after the murder, but she introduced herself to me as Martha Bell and claimed to be a waitress at the theatre. I soon discovered that no such person exists. Unfortunately, this brief distraction inadvertently led to me sending Mr Young to the coroner's office unaccompanied for the body identification process. In my lapse of judgment, I failed to realise that Mr Waters lacks the expertise to detect deception in such situations. I should have been personally present during this critical process, but I regretfully failed to do so.'

Timothy's gaze returned to the floor, the weight of his actions visibly wearing him down.

'Harry Denton, your manipulative ploys to keep your involvement hidden are exposed,' Matthews continued. 'You preyed on Bess and Timothy's vulnerability, using his and his wife's desperation as a means to further your own interests.'

Harry's expression twisted with a mix of guilt and shame, his facade crumbling.

'And Victor Crown,' Matthews concluded, his voice measured, 'you were an unwitting pawn in this dark game. Your mere association with Alice as more than an assistant set the stage for the tragedy that unfolded.'

Victor's face was a mask of disbelief, his world shattered by the revelation.

'This is preposterous!' Harry spat, his eyes blazing with fury. 'You can't seriously believe these accusations!' He looked at Victor with eyes wide and a vain throbbing in his forehead.

Matthews' gaze remained steady in the face of Harry's protests. 'The evidence speaks for itself, Mr Denton. The pieces of the puzzle have fallen into place, and the truth can no longer be concealed.'

Harry's chest heaved with frustration, his fists clenched at his sides. 'I had nothing to do with any of this! I had never even met Mr and Mrs Young before this ordeal. You're painting me as some sort of mastermind!' Harry Denton rose to his feet, kicking the chair behind him in frustration. 'I'm not going to sit around here and listen to this any longer. I'm leaving.'

Just as the tension reached its peak, a police officer re-appeared in the doorway, his expression resolute. 'Mr Denton, you are under arrest for your involvement in the death of Alice Grey.'

Harry's words caught in his throat as the gravity of the situation sank in. The officer stepped forward, his hand resting on the handcuffs at his belt. Harry's shoulders sagged, his defiance slowly giving way to a defeated resignation. He offered no further resistance as the officer secured the handcuffs around his wrists.

Timothy Young, his expression a mix of guilt and fear, stood beside Harry, his own fate now intertwined with that of his co-conspirator.

'Mr Young.' Matthews spoke before he was led out of the room. 'Where is Bess?'

'I honestly don't know.' Timothy sounded crushed.

As the officers led Harry and Timothy away, the weight of their actions hung heavily in the air. The room that had once been a haven of secrets and hidden agendas was now a stark reminder of the consequences of deceit.

Detective Matthews turned his attention to Victor Crown, who sat quietly, his shock still evident. 'Mr Crown,' Matthews began, his tone softer. 'You were unintentionally caught up in this web of deception.'

Victor nodded, his gaze distant. 'I can't believe... I had no idea... Why would he do this?'

'He was threatened by Alice. He thought his position was in trouble.'

'Why would he think such a thing? He has been my manager for so many years.'

'Mr Crown, were you aware that Alice Grey was

with child when she died?'

'I did not.' Victor's mouth fell open and his eyes bulged with shock.

'Well, Harry did.' Matthews spoke with care. 'You see, Harry tried to throw away many of Alice's items, including her diary, which he had tried to destroy, but we were able to read enough to suspect. Yesterday, I got confirmation in Mr Waters' coroner's report.'

Victor sat there in stunned silence, his mind clearly racing.

'You're free to go, Mr Crown,' Matthews informed him, acknowledging the illusionist's innocence in the scheme. 'And all the best with your final performances in town.' Victor nodded his acknowledgment as he slowly stood to leave.

'Harvey, would you mind taking Mr Crown back to his lodgings in the carriage, please?' Harvey nodded, and without saying a word, followed the illusionist out of the office.

EPILOGUE

FRIDAY 2ND DECEMBER 1892

Detective Benjamin Matthews walked home with Harvey, who had been invited around for an evening meal by Grace, to officially welcome his brother.

'It's been quite the week,' Harvey remarked as they walked the final bend to the house.

'Indeed, it has,' Matthews replied, ready for a relaxing evening and a good night's sleep.

As the two of them walked through the front door, the aroma of something delicious wafted through the air, and the sound of laughter and clinking glasses reached their ears. He stepped inside, shedding his coat and satchel, and followed the sounds of merriment to the living room.

Matthews was taken aback by Grace, his lovely wife, who was at the centre of it all, playing the gracious hostess role to perfection. Their living room had been transformed into an elegant cocktail party. The soft glow of candlelight danced upon the gilded picture frames and intricate wallpaper, as elegantly dressed guests mingled amidst the furniture, sipping from crystal glasses while the melodies of a piano wafted through the air, and a table was adorned with an array of hors d'oeuvres.

'Benjamin!' Grace exclaimed when she spotted him. She wore a radiant smile and glided over to give him a welcoming kiss. 'You're finally home.'

'What's all this?' Matthews replied, clearly taken aback by the unexpected party. 'And since when did we have a piano?'

'Oh, the neighbours loaned it to us for the evening. Isn't it wonderful?'

He couldn't help but smile. Grace had a knack for getting what she wanted, even at such short notice.
'I thought this was supposed to be just a little dinner for George and Harvey?'

'It was, but Lady Graham arrived this afternoon,

and one thing turned to another. Before I knew it, she was convincing me to have a celebratory party for the boys.'

Matthews laughed. 'So easily talked into things.'

The living room was filled with an eclectic mix of people, with Lady Graham talking to Harvey and George in the corner, and Charlotte and her husband with baby Hugo, sitting on the sofa. Clara Blackwell was also there, digging into the canapés and giving Matthews a little wave in acknowledgement. She had only called around to see Matthews after hearing the case was solved the day before and found herself invited in to join the party.

Matthews' friend Jack was also in attendance, hovering over the piano, which his wife, Beth, was playing beautifully in front of the bay window that had its long curtains closed.

'Let me introduce you to Lady Graham.' Grace pulled Matthews by the arm further into the living room and towards the brightly dressed woman before placing him in front of her and walking on to fetch more drinks. Matthews couldn't help but grin at her dumping him on a stranger.

'Lady Graham, I believe.' Matthews held out his

hand to shake hers.

'Oh, you must be the detective I've been hearing so much about.' Lady Graham beamed. 'George has been singing your praises for the past hour, and of course, that of your lovely wife. Not everyone would travel two days to help a young lad like Harvey search for his missing brother, no sir. Mark my words, you have a good egg there.'

Matthews tried to hide his grin, amused by her posh accent and eccentricity. 'It's good to finally meet you,' Matthews said. 'I'm thankful for the hospitality you showed my wife and Harvey at your home.'

'Oh, no trouble at all.' Lady Graham almost spilled her drink she was so excitable. 'To tell the truth, I enjoyed having them. If you ever feel the need to get out of town for the weekend, you are all more than welcome to stay with me.'

'Thank you. That is very kind. How long are you in Whitby?'

'I leave tomorrow, sadly, but I do like it here, so you never know, you may see me back!' She chuckled as though it was a humorous threat.

As the evening went on, Matthews found himself

engrossed in conversations with the various guests. Amidst the chatter and laughter, he couldn't help but feel grateful for this unexpected evening. He had spent so much of his time dealing with the darker aspects of life that he sometimes forgot the beauty and joy of the simpler things, such as spending an evening with those who were important to him.

Matthews found Clara in a quieter corner, surrounded by snacks with a glass in her hand. He cleared his throat, and she looked up with a warm smile.

'Clara,' he began. 'I wanted to thank you for your dedication to this case. Your insights and persistence have been invaluable.'

Clara's eyes sparkled with gratitude. 'Thank you, Detective. It's been quite the eye-opener.'

He leaned against the wall as he spoke to her, his tone earnest. 'If you ever decide that journalism isn't where you want to be, know that you'd be welcomed at the police department. Your investigative skills would be an asset.'

Clara's smile widened. 'I appreciate that, Detective. For now, though, I'll stick to the pen and paper. But I'm sure you will still see me around, especially if another case intrigues my investigative skills again.'

Matthews nodded, respect evident in his expression. 'Very well. Just know the offer stands.'

The hours melted away and the party showed no signs of winding down, but Benjamin's fatigue was catching up with him. He found himself a quiet spot on the sofa, and Grace quickly came over to join him.

'I'm looking forward to everybody leaving,' she whispered in his ear.

'Me too.' He kissed her on the cheek.

'I'm looking forward to us being alone.' She bit her bottom lip.

Matthews smiled, understanding her unspoken words. 'I see, Mrs Matthews. Well, I don't see why we can't just leave now,' he whispered back, a playful look in his eye.

She laughed and tapped him on the shoulder. 'We have guests.' She chuckled, yet her eyes remained looking directly into his.

A distinct knock at the front door sliced through the din of the party. It was a sharp, urgent rap, unlike the polite arrivals of their earlier guests. Heads turned, and the room fell momentarily silent as the unexpected interruption hung in the air.

Grace, her brow furrowed in confusion, looked at Matthews. 'Who could that be at this hour?'

'I'm not sure,' he replied, pushing himself up and rising to his feet. 'I'll go and check.'

With measured steps, Matthews left the room and reached for the front door. He opened it cautiously, revealing a figure that sent a ripple of surprise through him. Standing in the threshold, under the cover of night, was Victor Crown.

'Detective Matthews,' Victor said, his voice coarse. 'I'm sorry for the late hour. I hope I'm not interrupting anything.'

Matthews blinked in surprise but quickly stepped aside to allow Victor entry. 'Not at all, Mr Crown. Please, come in.'

Victor stepped into the warm hallway. 'I won't interrupt the party,' he said, holding back upon realising he had guests. 'I just finished my final show of the week, and I wanted to thank you, Detective, for helping to clear my name.'

'You have nothing to thank me for. The truth is

what cleared your name.'

'Well, I wanted to express my gratitude in person before I leave.'

'You're leaving this evening?'

'Yes, I think it's best.' He looked tired, his eyes heavy with dark circles underneath, his shoulders slouched from the weight of exhaustion. 'I have a long journey home, where I can have some rest before my next shows.'

'Well, it was an honour to meet you, Mr Crown.' Matthews held out his hand, and the illusionist shook it with a firm grip.

As Victor returned to the front door, he momentarily turned back to Matthews. 'Here, have this.' He handed the detective a small card, which Matthews took, thinking it to be a business card. However, within seconds of the card being in Matthews' palm, a small spark and puff of smoke emerged, and the card disappeared, leaving Matthews' hand empty. Victor, who did not look back, could be heard laughing to himself as he returned to his carriage.

Matthews, shaking his head and smiling with amusement, watched on as the carriage pulled away, leaving Whitby and never to return.

Detective Matthews

Book 4

Coming Soon!

If you enjoyed this Detective Matthews novel please do consider leaving a small review on Amazon or Goodreads.

Thank you

Behind The Scenes

Before releasing the first book in the Detective Matthews series, I knew it was going to be a multi-book series.

The interesting thing about this book, the third in the series, is that I had much of this plot and the characters we meet, fully formed in my mind before book one and two were completed.

I have always been a fan of the Victorian era, and most importantly this time when performers such as illusionists, mediums and magicians were really coming into their own. Although famous performer Harry Houdini found fame after the date this book is set in, there were still plenty of performers stunning crowds around the world.

In the modern day, we are now more skeptical of these kinds of performers, looking to debunk them, or expecting more extreme and dangerous kinds of performances.

One of my favourite modern performers is, Derren Brown. His ability to use mind tricks, misdirection and showmanship, in my opinion, puts him up there with the greats. I have had the privilege of seeing him perform live, and am in owe of his ability to recreate acts from the Victorian era, and bring them to a modern audience. If you haven't seen his stage work I would recommend them highly.

Incorporating an illusionist and theatre location into one of these stories was something I always knew I wanted to do, and I am thrilled with the outcome. I hope you enjoyed the story too.

Victorian Illusion

Victorian England was a time of great innovation and progress, and nowhere was this more evident than in the world of entertainment. Among the dazzling array of performers and shows that captivated the imaginations of Victorians, illusionists stood out as masters of mystery and marvel. These enigmatic performers, with their supernatural feats and mesmerizing tricks, held audiences in awe during the 19th century.

The Victorian era marked the golden age of illusionists, who were often referred to as "magicians" or "conjurers." They took the stage in ornate theaters and intimate parlors, captivating audiences with a mix of sleight of hand, optical illusions, and the clever use of props. Their performances often combined elements of science, artistry, and storytelling, creating an otherworldly experience for spectators.

One of the most famous illusionists of the time was John Nevil Maskelyne, who, along with his partner George Alfred Cooke, established the Egyptian Hall in London. The Egyptian Hall became the epicenter of magic in Victorian London, drawing crowds eager to witness Maskelyne and Cooke's astonishing illusions. Their performances included levitating tables, vanishing acts, and even the creation of ethereal apparitions that seemed to defy the laws of nature.

Another Victorian illusionist who left an indelible mark on the world of magic was Jean Eugène Robert-Houdin. Although he was French, Robert-Houdin's influence extended far beyond his home country. His elegant and refined style of performing contrasted with the more bombastic and flamboyant acts of the time. He introduced new technologies, such as electromagnetism, to create effects that baffled and astounded audiences.

Illusionists like Robert-Houdin and Maskelyne were not only entertainers but also inventors and innovators. They pushed the boundaries of what was possible, inspiring future generations of magicians and contributing to the development of modern magic.

Victorian-era illusionists were not without their controversies. Some claimed to possess supernatural powers, and their acts often blurred the line between science and superstition. Skeptics and debunkers emerged to challenge their claims, sparking debates about the authenticity of their performances.

Nevertheless, the allure of the Victorian illusionists was undeniable. They offered a form of escapism and wonderment to a society grappling with the rapid changes brought about by the Industrial Revolution. Their ability to transport audiences to a world of mystery and enchantment made them beloved figures of their time.

As we look back on the Victorian era, we remember these illusionists not only for their magical talents but also for their contributions to the history of entertainment. Their legacy continues to inspire and captivate audiences today, reminding us of the enduring power of illusion and the enduring appeal of the mysterious and the marvelous..

About The Author

Chris Turnbull was born in Bradford, West Yorkshire, before moving to Leeds with his family. Growing up with a younger brother, Chris was always surrounded by pets, from dogs, cats, rabbits and birds…the list goes on.

In 2012 Chris married his long term partner, since then Chris has relocated to the Yorkshire Wolds where he and his partner bought and renovated their first home together. Chris spends his free time writing, walking his dogs, and travelling as much as possible.

For more information about Chris and any future releases you can visit:

www.chris-turnbullauthor.com
facebook.com/christurnbullauthor
X: @ChrisTurnbull20
Instagram.com/Chris.Turnbull20

Acknowledgements

I would firstly like to thank my long suffering husband, who as always is so supportive of my writing projects, and is constantly being handed the next chapter to read for feedback.

I would also like the thank Karen Sanders for doing an excellent job with the editing and proofreading, and making the process enjoyable.

I would like to thank Joseph Hunt for the fantastic book cover design, it has been great fun working with you on the three 'D' book covers and now the Detective Matthews series.

Lastly I would like to thank all the people who have read and enjoyed my books, it is an honour to read your reviews and see that you are enjoying what I do too.

Thank You!

Printed in Great Britain
by Amazon